Shame on Me

TONYA CLARK

First time...

Shame on You

CHAPTER

One

ASHLYN

ALL THE FOOTBALL GAMES, dances, friendships gained and lost, heartbreaks, first loves, worry over grades, or just in general the high school drama, it all comes down to this one night. Graduation.

High School hasn't been bad for me. I have a small group of friends and we spent our high school years in the middle of the pack. Not the popular jocks, but not the book nerds either.

Yesterday, I would have told you the last four years seemed to crawl. Today, it feels like just yesterday I walked onto the campus as a freshman. Looking now at my reflection in the full-length mirror, it's hard to believe I'm standing here in my cap and gown.

Along the wooden frame of my mirror are pictures outlining my last four years. Pictures of Hannah, my best friend, and our small group ready for the dances. The day I passed my driver's license test. Days of summer spent at the beach, but at the top is my favorite picture. I'm sandwiched in between my brother, Jackson, and his best friend, Kayson. It's the day they both left for bootcamp the summer before my freshman year.

They have been best friends for as long as I can remember. I grew up with two protective brothers. My little secret, I don't think I ever looked at Kayson like a brother, I think I've had a crush on him since I decided boys didn't have cooties.

Jackson and I have always been close. Four years separate our age and there is nothing more that I would want but for him to be here for tonight, but he will be home in two weeks and then we have the summer. In the four years he has been in the military he has only been home once and that was two years ago. Last time he talked to Mom and Dad he informed them he wasn't reenlisting, so he will be home to stay this time. It may not be tonight, but I'll take it.

A knock at my door has me quickly blinking to keep the tears back that are threatening to fall, plus I don't normally wear a lot of makeup and have to remember mascara and tears don't mix.

"I know, I'm coming." I grab my cap off my head, grab my phone and reach for my door.

Quickly throwing my bedroom door open, nothing could have prepared me for the sight on the other side. Standing there looking proud in his military uniform is Jackson. It's like he morphed out of my mind and just appeared. There are no words, no movement, just complete shock.

Mascara is done for. Tears instantly rush my eyes, it's like those videos all over social media of soldiers coming home. I cry every time I watch one of those, only this time my tears are for my brother. I launch myself at him, for I have no words on how much this means to me that he is here.

His arms wrap tight around me, "Come on, Ash, did you honestly think I would miss this?"

Nodding my head is all I can do to answer him, because I believed him when he told me he couldn't be home for a couple more weeks. I just spoke to him last night.

"Is it my turn yet?" The deep voice instantly puts butterflies in my stomach.

My brother's arms loosen from around me and my feet hit the floor. Turning toward the voice I have dreams about, I can't believe my eyes when they land on Kayson, also in uniform.

Without thinking I launch myself into his arms, my legs wrapping around his waist. His arms hold me tight. I know now why I haven't dated the last four years. My heart belongs to this guy, unfortunately I'm looked at by him as just the little sister.

I don't want to let go, but I know I have to. Getting my legs and arms to obey is tough, but I finally manage to release my hold on him. When his arms fall away from me, I have to fight the need to wrap myself back around him.

"I can't believe you guys didn't tell me you were coming home." I wipe at the tears running down my face.

"What, and miss this look?" My brother's hand waves in the direction of my face.

Crap, I can only image what I look like, and this is the first thing Kayson sees after two years.

I try to wipe under my eyes, but I'm thinking it's a lost cause by the expression on my brother's face.

"Hurry up and clean up, Mom sent us up here to get you moving."

I don't want to let them out of my sight for fear that this is a dream and the next time I come out of my room, they won't be here. My brother and I have been close our whole lives, only seeing him once in the last four years has been heartbreaking.

"Let's get a move on it." Dad's voice travels up the stairs.

"Don't move, I'll be right back." I instruct both of them as I turn back into my room, leaving the door open so that I can see them the entire time.

Using a makeup removing cloth I quickly clean up my raccoon eyes and apply a new coat of mascara. Looking behind me in the mirror, both Jackson and Kayson stand there. Jackson is saying something to Kayson, but what, I have no idea. The only thing I'm seeing is Kayson's eyes, staring right back at me in the mirror. Something shifts in my chest and I have to tell myself it's nothing. Those green eyes are just something I wish would look at me as more than maybe the kid sister of his best friend.

"What's keeping everyone up there? You'll have plenty of time to catch up tonight at dinner." Mom's voice is the next to rush me from downstairs.

Kayson blinks a couple times and then looks away, responding to what ever my brother has said.

Last look, it will have to do. "Come on, guys, I'm ready." Sliding an arm around each of theirs, I'm once again sandwiched between them, just like the picture four years ago.

JOINING the class as we prepare to walk into graduation, I find Hannah. We have been best friends since junior high.

"I get being happy about this but your smile is beyond happy to graduate, what's causing it?" Hannah knows me way too well.

"Jackson and Kayson are home." I find myself bobbing on my tippy-toes.

"What? I thought they weren't home for another couple of weeks."

Nodding, I can't seem to wipe the smile off my face. "I know."

"So, tell me. How does Kayson look?"

I don't know who she thinks she is fooling. I know the real person she is interested in is Jackson. I swore before my brother left the only reason she was my friend was because she was able to spend time at my house with my brother.

At the mention of Kayson's name I try to control my smile from getting bigger. Shrugging, I try to play it off, "He looks about the same really."

Hannah rolls her eyes, "Please, you haven't given any guy here at school the time of day. Not sure who you think you are fooling but it isn't me."

THE CEREMONY SEEMS to be dragging by. The endlessly long speeches that, if it wasn't for the excitement of walking across that stage and grabbing a diploma, the whole group of us down here would have fallen asleep during. I'm not sure how long we have been sitting here, feels like hours, but finally we are starting to file up to receive the last piece of our high school existence.

My name is called and it is unmistakable where my family is located in the large stadium. They are up on their feet, yelling and clapping, but I won't lie, the only person I see is Kayson.

Caps are thrown in the air, the stadium erupts with watching families and that's it, we are officially high school graduates. I find Hannah first and together we search out our families in a sea of people now filling the field.

Tight arms wrap around me from behind and I'm lifted off the ground. Hannah's eyes brighten and I know instantly who it is. I knew she had a thing for my brother.

"Proud of you, Ash," his voice booms behind me.

"I need to get some pictures." Mom has tears in her eyes.

In rotation we spend the next hour or so getting pictures with family and my friends as I find them.

STRETCHING my hand over the back of the front passenger seat, I ask, "Mom, can I see your phone and the pictures you took?"

Flipping through them, I come upon the one of Kayson and I. Him in his uniform, myself in the graduation gown. His arm around my shoulders pulling me in tight to his side, my arms wrapped around his waist, but what tops it off is that he is kissing me on the forehead. To him I know it's nothing different than what my brother would do, to me it's wishing he looked at me like the woman I have grown into, not the little kid that I believe he still sees me as.

I can't help but look for the little differences, though. My brother's arm around my shoulders is just laying there, Kayson holds me tightly to his side. When they surprised me at the house, Jackson hugged me tight, yes, but Kayson, I would have sworn I felt his hand move up and down my back. His eyes looking back at me through the mirror, though, that's what keeps running through my head. I know I'm probably making more out of all of this than I should, but seeing him in his uniform after two years, if anything this crush I have on him has only become more intense.

CHAPTER
Two

KAYSON

SHE IS my best friend's little sister and I'm pretty sure Jackson would kick me in the ass right now if he knew what has been flying through my head tonight.

I will admit, most of our friendship, even up to the day we both left for boot camp, I looked at Ashlyn like the little sister I didn't have. I'm an only child and always wanted siblings. Jackson and Ashlyn were very close and I always envied that. When we left for the Marines she was just starting high school.

Jackson and I have been together for the past four years serving in the same platoon. Two years ago, after one of our tours we were able to request a leave and returned home after two years of being gone. I will never forget that day. Ashlyn came running out of the house and jumped right into my arms. My chest tightened a little when her body crashed against mine. My arms had a mind of their own and didn't want to let her go, the only thing that pried them from her body was Jackson's voice.

"Excuse me, I believe I'm home as well."

I couldn't believe at that time how much she had changed, but that was minor compared to the woman I had jumping into my arms tonight. Or the longing I saw in her eyes earlier in the mirror. I'm trying to convince myself that it's because we have been out in the desert, no real opportune times to be around the opposite sex, but I know that is just an excuse so that I don't have to tell my best friend that I think I have fallen for his kid sister.

"After dinner with the family, do you want to go and get a drink or something?" Jackson breaks through my thoughts.

"Not going to lie, man, I'm good with just staying in tonight and relaxing."

"Well, Mike found out we are back in town and text me during the graduation asking if we wanted to hit that country bar in town. I kind of already told him we would. I was going to stay in with Ashlyn tonight but Mom said she is going to a graduation party after dinner with Hannah, so I figured why stay home? Dancing, beer, and women sounded a little more exciting."

Staying in isn't sounding as good now knowing Ashlyn won't be there. I need to get my head back on straight anyway.

"All right, I'll need you to drop me off at home on the way back to change, though."

DINNER WAS two hours too long. Ashlyn sat herself right between her brother and myself. Nothing out of the ordinary really, but her leg touching mine had me jumping slightly in my chair. What surprised me even more is when I realized it was me that made the move, on the other hand she didn't move away either. I had to keep both hands on top of the table to keep myself from placing one of them on her knee.

I didn't miss the looks she gave me every now and then but I was never more thankful than when Hannah mentioned it was time for her and Ashlyn to leave. They were leaving from dinner to go straight to the party.

Jackson and I excused ourselves right after to head out and change to meet up with Mike and a couple of guys.

THE BAR IS PACKED. I'm nursing my second beer, but I've lost count on how many Jackson has finished off. He hasn't left the dance floor with one of the ladies he met the moment we walked in. Myself, I have turned down a number of dance invitations and have kept this bar stool warm the entire night. I'm starting to think I should have stayed in tonight.

My phone vibrates in my pocket, setting my beer on the table I stand to see who could be texting me. My parents are at a dinner party tonight and Jackson is here.

Ashlyn: I can't get ahold of Jackson, I need someone to come pick me up please.

Scanning the dance floor I find Jackson. Weaving myself through the couples two-stepping, I get Jackson's attention.

"Ashlyn has been trying to call you, she needs us to pick her up."

The woman with Jackson starts to pout, "You are leaving already?"

"Give me the car keys. I'll go and get her, you can grab a ride with Mike, or text me and I'll come and pick you up later."

Jackson doesn't even hesitate. Pulling the keys out of his pocket he tosses them to me, "Thanks, man. I owe you one."

Waving him off like it's no big deal, I make my way off the dance floor and out to the car. Once inside, I pull my phone out and reply to Ashlyn's text.

Me: Where are you? I'm on my way.

Instantly she responds with an address.

PULLING UP TO THE HOUSE, it brings back the memories of our high school parties. Everyone is drunk and acting like there isn't a care in the world. No idea of what reality and the real world holds. There were times in the desert I wished I could have these care-free days back.

Finding a place down the street to park, I make my way up to the loud music, maneuvering through the young, drunk girls' grabby hands, and being rammed into a few times by drunk guys pushing each other around. Oh, the days!

These are the moments I'm thankful for being taller than most, helps in the search through the sea of heads.

It takes a few minutes, but I finally spot Ashlyn. From here I can see the irritation in her eyes for the guy who has one hand planted on the wall by her head, probably more for stability for his drunken state but trying to play it off as looking cool.

As I get closer I hear her voice, "Sean, back off. I told you I'm not interested. I'm waiting on someone else."

That's my cue. I receive a little too much pleasure in pushing the guy aside to make myself known. I have no idea what possesses me to do what I did next.

"Sorry I'm late." Grabbing her behind the head, I claim Ashlyn's lips with my own.

I feel her body stiffen against mine, I'm sure from the shock of my action, but what surprises me more is it doesn't take long for her body to relax and before I can stop, she is kissing me back.

CHAPTER
Three

ASHLYN

SEAN IS DRIVING ME CRAZY. For the past hour he has been following me around. This is my reason for wanting to leave the party, problem is, Hannah is having the time of her life and I feel bad asking her to leave. I tried Jackson more than once, when that didn't work I tried Kayson. Thankfully he answered and is on his way, I just wish he would hurry. Each time I have found a different place to relocate to, to wait for Kayson to get here, Sean has been there as well and each time getting a little closer and closer. I know he is drunk. His words are slurred, his breath reeks, his eyes are glassed over and heavily hooded and he needs to hold onto the wall to keep himself up. There is nothing about him right now that is slightly attractive. He is definitely in my personal space and my nerves are starting to get the best of me, in a minute I'm going to get louder and everyone is going to know how annoying he is being.

The relief I feel at seeing Kayson push his way between us causes me to slump against the wall in relief. Nothing could have prepared me for his next actions.

His fingers push through my hair at the back of my head and before I can even guess his intentions, his lips are on mine. It's not a small peck, there is nothing "friendly" about the way his lips are demanding mine to respond. This has to be a dream, this has only happened in my dreams, but as my one hand come up to his chest and I feel the warmth of his skin through his shirt, I realize my dreams are reality. Fisting his shirt in my hand to keep him from moving away, I bring my other one up to the nape of his neck and before I can stop myself, I'm kissing him back.

I hear no loud music, I have no care in the world if Sean is standing there watching us, or who may be seeing this. All I know at the moment is that when Kayson's other arm wraps around my waist and pulls me tight against him, I may have moaned a little.

Time has been lost. I have no idea how long we have been standing here kissing, but I instantly feel the loss when he ends the kiss. For a quick moment our eyes hold each other's, but I can't read his. I have no idea what may be going through his head right now.

"Are you ready to go?" His voice sounds distant to my foggy brain, but somehow I manage to answer him with a nod of my head.

Grabbing my hand, Kayson starts to weave us through all of my classmates, on a path to the front door.

Making our way outside, I'm hoping the night air will be inviting and refreshing, but the summer heat is already here and there is nothing cooling me down.

Kayson hasn't said a word. He just continues to walk, holding my hand tightly, as we are basically in a slow run down the street to what I'm assuming is where he parked.

Walking up to my brother's car, I finally find my voice, "Why do you have Jackson's car?"

"We met up with some of the guys. He wasn't ready to go, so I took the car to come pick you up."

Opening the passenger door for me, his hand releases mine and it's everything I can do not to reach for his again. Without even looking up at him, I take my seat in the car, him shutting the door for me.

I watch as he rounds the front of the car. He stands outside of the driver's side door for a moment before he actually opens the door, folding himself into the driver's seat. He seems a little irritated, maybe he wasn't ready to leave either, or maybe I interrupted something that was going on wherever he was.

"Look, I'm sorry. I didn't mean to ruin your evening by having you come and pick me up. I tried calling and texting Jackson but he never answered. Hannah was having a good time and I was ready to leave."

"He is too drunk to drive anyway."

He hasn't looked at me since getting into the car, his hands are gripping the steering wheel and I can see his knuckles change to a lighter color as his hands flex around it. Kayson is mad. I made him leave whatever he had going on wherever he was, and then he has to save me from a drunken idiot at a party. The high I was feeling a few minutes ago sinks fast and now all I want is to be home, in my room away from everyone. I feel like such a fool.

My phone vibrates in my pocket. Pulling it out, I have a text from Hannah.

Hannah: Did I just see you kissing Kayson?

I can't answer her, I'm too embarrassed right now. Shoving my phone back in my pocket, I sink down into the seat as though I'm trying to disappear into it. Kayson starts the car and pulls onto the street.

I was expecting us to stop and pick up Jackson from wherever he is, but instead I find myself sitting in a car with Kayson, along the curb in front of my house, in silence.

For the first time ever, I have no words. I have never felt awkward around Kayson and I've done some pretty embarrassing things, but right now I feel like if I speak I'll say the wrong thing or embarrass myself royally.

We can't sit out here in the car all night either. I'm just going to say thank you for picking me up and exit the vehicle.

Reaching for the door handle, I refuse to look over at him for I'm sure my cheeks are still bright pink from our earlier kiss. "Thank you for picking me up, sorry you had to leave the guys." I hurry to open the door.

Kayson's hand wraps around my arm, stopping me from moving out of the car, "Ash, wait!"

Here we go, the talk I'm not ready to have. I'm happy with getting out of this car believing Kayson only kissed me to keep the very drunk Sean away from me. I'm okay with saying thank you, going up to my room, replaying the moment over and over in my head for the night and then acting like nothing happened the next time I see him.

Maybe if I talk first, it will make this a less awkward for me. "Kayson, thank you for helping out tonight, Sean was pretty drunk and I couldn't seem to shake him. Again, I'm sorry if I ruined your night out with the guys. I'm sure after getting home from being gone for so long that the last thing you wanted to do was rescue your best friend's little sister."

"First off, stop apologizing for asking for a ride. No one should have to stay where they are feeling uncomfortable. Second, you are more than just Jackson's little sister, Ash."

More than just Jackson's sister? What is that supposed to mean? I try not to allow myself hope that just maybe, Kayson has felt a little more for me than just the annoying sister.

CHAPTER
Four

KAYSON

I SEE the questions flying through Ashlyn's eyes as she searches mine for answers. What the hell am I doing?

I'm a guy and would be lying if I said that I never noticed Ashlyn as more than just the little sister of my best friend. Any guy who doesn't notice her is either not into girls, or blind. That four-year gap, however, in high school is a large gap, especially when I was leaving for the military and she was just stepping foot into high school. To top it off, she is Jackson's little sister, that has always been a very large, red stop sign.

My intentions when I saw that kid a little too close to Ashlyn were just to walk up, ask if she was ready and then lead her out of the party. Something switched when I walked up and her eyes met mine. There was relief, and a little pleading to help her out of the situation she was in. Not sure why I thought kissing her was the help she needed, and I never intended for it to be that kind of kiss. My plan was a little kiss on the lips, wrap my arm around the shoulders, pull her in tight to my side and make sure the drunk guy got the hint that she wasn't interested.

However, when my lips touched hers and I heard that little shocked intake of breath, something switched. What sealed it was when the initial shock wore off and she started kissing me back. It took everything in me not to go all caveman and throw her over my shoulder, carrying her out for all to see she belongs to me.

The response she gave me was a sure sign that she was wanting that kiss as much as I was, and right now even though she is trying very hard to act as though it was no big deal that we just kissed less than an hour ago, I see it in her eyes that she wouldn't stop me if I did it again.

Her eyes, as much as she tries to keep them up at mine, keep looking down at my lips, and the light green depths of them have turned to a brighter green. I have no idea what I'm doing about this past tonight, or what I will say to Jackson, but right now all I can really think about is the way her eyes have that wishful look in them.

Unhooking my seatbelt with one hand, I pull her over the center of the car with the hand that already has a grip on her arm, bringing those lips back to mine. She doesn't resist, she meets my lips with hers and for the second time tonight I'm lost.

An earlier conversation flashes through my head, and that's the cold water I needed thrown on me at this exact moment. I have no right kissing Ashlyn, I'm leaving on Monday.

Pulling away from her is hard, but the right thing to do. Actually we are far past the "right thing to do," I should never have kissed her to begin with, and definitely not a second time.

When her eyes open and look at me they have a dreamy look. All I want to do is bring her back into my arms, but the right thing to do is walk away. I'm moving out of state in a couple of days and no one knows about it yet, not even Jackson. I have taken a firefighter job in the state of Washington.

I wasn't expecting to be getting into a position this quickly, but maybe it's for the best. Two kisses from Ashlyn and I'm about to call back and tell them I'm not taking the job. Ashlyn isn't the kind of girl a guy can walk away from easily. She is smart, funny, strong-minded, giving and caring. Even though I know she can take care of herself, I can't help but want to protect her, always have.

"Is everything all right?" Her voice is low, but her eyes show the concern and again there is that look of uncertainty.

Nodding, I pull back and put a little space between the two of us, she follows my lead and sits back into the passenger seat. "I need to go and pick up Jackson."

It's a lie, but I need to leave before I do something I will really regret, like beg her to come with me.

Ashlyn doesn't need that kind of tie down. She has just graduated high school and needs to start the next chapter of her life in college. I have no idea what she even wants to do for a career, that's how little we have talked in the past four years.

We both have new chapters in our lives beginning, this isn't the time to start anything for either of us.

CHAPTER
Five

ASHLYN

I'M NOT sure what is going on, but I know Kayson as well as I know my brother and something isn't being said.

I want to keep pushing him, but I know he isn't going to tell me anything if he isn't wanting to, one thing about Kayson, very strong-minded. Right now, though, I'm extremely confused on what's going on.

After the first time he kissed me I could have easily moved on and thought it was just his way of protecting me from an unwanted advance from a very drunk class-mate. The second kiss, though, what am I supposed to think of that one? There was no need for that one, which leads me to believe that he was wanting it.

Right now, as much as I want to ask the questions flying through my head, I'm taking the fact that he is staring straight out the windshield and his hands are in his lap as a sign that he isn't wanting to talk.

"All right, well, thank you again for picking me up tonight, I really appreciate it."

His head bobs but that is the only response I get. I'm not going to sit and wait him out for an explanation. Pushing the car door open, I make my way out and shut it behind me. The moment it shuts, Kayson puts the car in gear and pulls away from the curb.

I refuse to have him look back and see me standing here, so I quickly turn and make my way up the walkway and into the house. It's late, thankfully, so my parents are both probably in bed and I don't have to worry about any questions of how my night was.

I'M NOT sure how long I laid in bed before I finally fell asleep, but every time my phone vibrated with an incoming message I would jump and my heart would leap in my chest thinking that Kayson was texting to explain, or something. Nope, each time it was Hannah asking again about me kissing Kayson, then about if I made it home all right. That one I answered so that she wouldn't worry, but the rest I left un-responded. Which only drove her to text more but I ignored those as well.

A couple of times I had started a text to Kayson, but then decided against it. I'm not one of those girls. If he has something to say to me, he knows where to find me.

• • •

BY MORNING I have decided that this is all a little ridiculous and being two adults we should be able to talk about what happened last night.

Both Mom and Dad have left for work already when Jackson comes home looking like he hadn't slept at all last night and still looking a little drunk. I'm enjoying myself a nice bowl of cereal when he plops down in the stool next to me, his forehead going straight down onto the counter.

"Rough night?"

HIs head turns and bloodshot eyes glare up at me.

"I would have thought you'd have grown out of the whole 'drinking and partying all night' phase of your life?"

"Yep, me too, but I guess I had one more round left."

"Did you stay at Kayson's last night after he picked you up?"

"Kayson didn't pick me up. I rode home with Mike, he just dropped me off." Pulling his large frame up off the stool, he stands, "Now if you will excuse me I think, I'm going to go lie down for a while."

I watch as he walks up the stairs and I have to admit my heart drops a little in my chest. Kayson didn't leave to go and pick up my brother, he just used that excuse to get away from me.

Pulling my phone out of my pocket, I find Kayson's name and open a text conversation.

Me: We need to talk.

I expected to have him ignore me, so I'm really surprised when a response instantly comes back from him.

Kayson: I'll be over soon.

Nerves start to boil up in my stomach. We need to talk, but what is going to be said is a little unnerving.

The girl who has secretly had a crush on him since I can remember is bouncing up and down in hopes that he feels the same way. The realistic side of me is afraid he will tell me it was all a mistake, just caught up in a moment or something.

I'M SITTING in the living room when Kayson walks into the house. Walking over, he sits in the chair across from me. Silence stretches between us, and the nerves I have been feeling all morning have only intensified now.

From the look on his face, I can tell this isn't going to go the way I was hoping. I'm seeing the regret in his eyes and it is breaking my heart. I have to fight to keep myself from leaving the room altogether.

"Ash, all the way over I was thinking of what I wanted to say, actually it's been on my mind all night. I'm just going to say it…"

Holding up my hand, I stop him, "Kayson, I'm not the little girl that has followed you around since I was five, I know what you are going to say."

"No, I'm pretty sure you don't. I'm moving out of state in a couple of days."

He's right, that wasn't what I was expecting him to say. "Out of state, where?"

"Washington, I got a job up there at one of the fire stations, I found out yesterday."

"You just got home."

"I know. Trust me, surprised me as much as you right now. It's what I want to do, so I'm going."

"So you knew when you came and picked me up last night. You knew when you kissed me not only once, but twice?"

"That wasn't planned. When I saw that guy in your space last night and the look on your face, I reacted. Then you kissed me back."

"So this is my fault?"

"No, but when you kissed me back I realized how much I liked it. It felt right. Then the asshat in me couldn't just have one, I wanted the second one. I want you."

"You want me? Only for the next couple of days and then you are leaving?" Tears are burning the backs of my eyes, but I'm refusing to let Kayson see them.

I have nothing else to say to him, my heart is broken and the one guy I have had on a pedestal in my mind for most of my life has just let me down.

"Shame on me for believing in you more."

"Ash, come on, don't…"

"Don't what? I'm grown up enough to admit I have feelings for you, Kayson. Maybe what I should be saying is shame on you for never seeing them."

"Ash, what do you want me to do here? Admit that I care? All right, I care, but that doesn't change anything. I'm moving in two days."

I'm going to be the one to walk away from him. "Good-bye, Kayson."

Second time...

Shame on Me

CHAPTER

Six

ASHLYN

LOOKING down the line of lockers in front of me, I'm having a very hard time containing myself from doing a happy dance right here in the station's bay. It's been a long three years, but I'm here. That's my last name over that locker and across the back of my gear.

Three years ago, I decided to become a firefighter. My parents, I think, were too shocked to say anything to try and change my mind and my brother, well, Jackson just thought I was chasing after the only guy I had ever loved. As much as I argued that he was wrong, deep down I have to admit, it might have had a little to do with it. It didn't help my argument when I announced that I was moving here to California to go to school either, same state as that same guy moved to.

I've worked hard the last three years, lots of training, lots of studying, and finally today is the day, my first day here at my new fire station. My hands fisted at my sides, I find myself no longer able to control a little bounce in the hips as I allow myself a very small happy dance. I deserve it.

"Hi…" A voice behind me causes me to jump and turn quickly, all the while trying to keep my face averted down because I can feel that my cheeks have warmed up a bit from embarrassment from being caught in the middle of my very slight celebration dance.

"I promise I won't tell anyone." The guy waves a hand confirming my fear, I was caught in my happy dance.

With my hand I indicate to the locker behind me, "It's my first day. As embarrassing as it is that you caught me, I have to admit, I'm excited."

Holding his hand out to me, he introduces himself. "I'm Neil, my first day as well. Won't lie, I did my own little dance over by my locker."

Shaking his hand, my body relaxes some. "Nice to meet you, Neil, I'm Ashlyn."

"It's nice to meet you. I just thought I would introduce myself. I'll leave you to your dancing."

Before I can say anything to him, the large doors of the garage begin to open and the station's engine and ladder trucks begin to back in.

"I guess they are back, time to meet the crew."

Neil doesn't seem nervous at all. I'm just hoping the nerves that are racking my entire body right now aren't visible.

The back door to the engine cab flies open before it's parked. "What the hell are you doing here?"

The firefighter jumps out, still wearing his turnout pants, suspenders up over the station t-shirt. There is no way I'm seeing what I am. If I thought my feelings for this man were gone, I was very wrong. Nothing could have prepared me for the rocket of emotion that shoots through my body when I realize who that voice belongs to. Out of all the stations in California, how did I end up in the exact same house as him?

It's been three years since I've heard that voice or seen that face. I've spent most of my life in love with one guy, Kayson, my brother's best friend. My freshman year of high school both he and my brother decided they needed to serve their country. Four years later they both surprised me for my high school graduation by coming home. The real surprise came later that night, when the one guy I had dreamt about kissing me did just that when he came and picked me up from a graduation party, only to tell me the next day it was a mistake and that he was moving to California to take a job as a firefighter. I haven't seen him since. Now here he is, stalking up to me like I have no business being here.

What surprises me more than seeing Kayson is that just before Kayson reaches me, Neil, the new guy, steps in front of me, putting himself between me and Kayson, stopping him in his charge toward me.

Well, there goes my happy dance mood.

As much as I appreciate Neil's protective gesture, I need to prove to everyone here that I can stand on my own two feet, and hiding behind him isn't a good start to that. Plus, I don't need protection physically from Kayson; emotionally, that's something different.

Stepping out from behind Neil, I move to stand almost toe to toe with Kayson. My breath catches as I get a good look at him. The last three years have only made the guy I once thought to be the hottest guy ever, even more attractive. My heart begins to slam in my chest as I try to control the emotions that I would have sworn I had in check when it came to this man.

Kayson gives me a once over as his eyes take in the uniform that I'm wearing. There is no denying that I'm a firefighter at this station and I can see him trying to register this information. I'm starting to think that Jackson never told Kayson what I was doing after he left.

It's at this moment I realize that I have really missed him. It takes everything in me not to jump into his arms and hug him. Yes, I might not have liked how he left, but this man has been in my life for most of it and I'm realizing how much I've missed him.

"This is a joke, right?" His eyes roam my uniform in disbelief.

Need to hug him, gone.

"Hey, man, what's your problem?" Neil comes to my rescue once again but from behind me this time.

The rest of the crew has joined the scene now and I start to feel my cheeks heat up from embarrassment. I'm literally sandwiched in between two guys. Probably not the best way to start my first day.

My temper starts to flare now. I've worked way too hard to make it in this career, to prove that I have what it takes to stand alongside these men and do the job. I'll be damned if I'm going to allow any man in this station, be it the nice new guy or the jackass who broke my heart, to try and prove that I can't take care of myself.

Turning to Neil, I try to speak nicely, none of this is his fault. "Neil, thank you, but I have this. He is an old family friend."

Now I turn my attention back to Kayson, him I have to stop my urge to slap. Instead, I hold out my hand, and give what I hope to be a sarcastically sweet smile. "Hello, I'm Ashlyn, the new firefighter at this station."

Kayson looks down at my hand as though it's a snake that's about to strike at him. His eyes meet with mine again, "Why?"

Dropping my hand, I shrug, "It turns out, I'm very good at this job."

I catch movement coming up from behind Kayson. The man approaching is tall, older than the rest, I would say by the slight streaks of silver outlining his hairline maybe late forties. "Is there a problem here, Shaw?" The man uses Kayson's last name.

Kayson takes a deep breath before his stance relaxes a little, "No, Cap, everything is fine."

Of course, this man would be the captain, now I really want to punch Kayson.

Taking a deep breath, I straighten my shoulders a little more and turn my attention to my new captain. "Hello, I'm Ashlyn Murphy."

"Murphy, yes," he looks over my shoulder, "and you must be Walker. I welcome both of you to Station 26. I'm Captain Brett Mitchell."

"Thank you," both Neil and I respond at the same time.

"We better show you two around before another call comes in. Cowboy, would you take Neil and show him the ropes and…"

"I've got Murphy," Kayson interrupts the captain.

It's on the tip of my tongue to argue with him, but there has been enough attention on me today, I really just want to get ready for my first shift.

The captain eyes Kayson for a moment, but then nods his head, "Fine, get her settled in. I'll chat with both of you once you're finished."

Kayson gives me a cocky smile, "Let's go."

I just roll my eyes at him.

Grabbing my bag from the bench in front of my locker, I follow Kayson up a flight of stairs into a great room style living room and kitchen. He doesn't say a word, as

I follow him around I try to mentally take notes of where everything is. We stop at a door, he opens it and steps aside for me to go in first. Walking past him, I try very hard not to touch him as I enter the room.

It's a small room with three partition walls and four beds, each with their own nightstand next to it. Then along the wall with the door are lockers I'm going to assume are used for closets. It's a plain room but I wasn't expecting anything different.

To my right I notice another door. Pointing, I ask, "Bathroom?"

Kayson just nods. He hasn't said a word to me since down in the bay. Setting my bag down, I turn to him, my arms crossed at my chest, "If you have something to say, just say it."

He just stares at me for a moment, I can see him battling with himself on what he shouldn't or should say. Finally, he steps into the room and shuts the door. "Why didn't you tell me?"

Is he joking right now? He hasn't spoken to me in three years and he just asked me why I didn't tell him. "I didn't realize I needed to let you know what my life plans were, you sure didn't think it was important to have me part of yours."

"I didn't even know you were studying to be a fire-fighter."

"That just proves you didn't care enough to ask," I shoot back.

Kayson closes the space between us, his arm wrapping around my waist and pulling me tight to him, his lips only inches from mine. "You have no idea about my feelings for you."

Having my body so tightly pressed to his is playing with all kinds of my feelings. It is taking everything I have not to melt into his arms, but he left me without any further communication. "You're right, I don't. How could I? You kissed me and then left."

My eyes challenge his, daring him to say anything else. He knows I'm right. His eyes bounce between my lips and my eyes and for a split moment I think he is going to kiss me, but instead his arm pulls back from around me as though I've slapped him and he pushes away. Relief and disappointment wash over me all at once. This isn't something I can allow to happen. Whatever I wanted to happen three years ago is in the past and I've moved on, I can't fall down that hole again, I barely made it out the last time. Kayson Shaw shattered my heart. First time shame on you…if I allowed it to happen again, it would be shame on me.

"It was a kiss, Ashlyn."

It feels like that one little statement just shattered my heart all over again. "Yes, Kayson, you're right, it was a kiss and for you that may have been all it was, but for the girl who had been in love with you most of my life, it was more, so much more."

I need to get out of this small area with him all around me. I'm no longer that naive high school girl, I don't want to stand here and have this battle with him. What happened was in the past, we both moved on, now we just need to find a way to work together.

Moving past him, I open the door and leave him standing there. Turning before I head back to the others, I add, "All we have to do is our jobs, Kayson, I promise you I'm not expecting anything else." With that I walk away from him this time.

CHAPTER

Seven

KAYSON

I'M PISSED AT MYSELF, she's my best friend's sister and the woman who has been haunting my dreams every night for the past three years.

When we returned this morning from our call, my eyes instantly locked onto the woman standing in the bay as we pulled in. I even blinked a couple of times to make sure I was seeing correctly. Ashlyn was standing there, with another guy. What didn't register at first was the station uniform she was wearing. When that guy stepped in front of her acting as though he needed to protect her from me, I assumed he was a boyfriend. It didn't click until he moved to the side and I noticed they were both wearing a station uniform.

This is insane, how did I not know that she was training to be a firefighter? Why didn't Jackson think to mention that she had moved to California? Damn, the guy has been here to visit a number of times and never once did he mention Ashlyn; of course, I hadn't asked either.

Jackson gave me the silent treatment for a couple of days after he found out I kissed his kid sister. I may have thought about her a lot, but never did I bring her up with him. I was just thankful I didn't lose my best friend.

I still can't wrap my brain around the fact that she has been this close the whole time and I had no idea. Out of all the stations she could have ended up at, she is here at mine.

Pulling my phone out of my pocket, I open up a text with Jackson.

Me: Seriously, no heads up?

Hitting send, I know that he will understand what I'm saying, asshat.

Just as my phone vibrates with a response from Jackson, my captain shows up in the hallway. I'm still standing in the doorway of the room that I just showed Ashlyn to.

Cap makes his way to me. "Shaw, everything good?"

"Yep."

Cap eyes me for a moment. "You have previously known our new firefighter, I'm assuming?"

Nodding, I answer, "Only since she was about four. Ashlyn is my best friend's sister."

His eyes widen slightly, "And you had no idea she was coming here?"

This time I shake my head, "Nope."

"I'm going to assume there is more to this story than just the best friend's sister judging by the fist you were about to plant into the new guy's face."

The whole station doesn't need to know that I was an ass for allowing Ashlyn to get away, I have already smacked myself upside the head many times since that day I left her house.

"Just surprised is all. I have no problems with the new guy. I'm good."

Captain eyes me for a moment and I can see that he is trying to assess how much to believe of what I've said. "All right, for now I won't ask any more questions, just remember we all have to work together as a team here."

I fight the need to roll my eyes, Cap knows me better than that. "I can swear to you, nothing would come before the safety of everyone."

"I know, just a friendly reminder." With that said and a look that tells me he isn't buying my denial of something between Ashlyn and myself, he turns and walks back down the hall, leaving me once again alone.

Bringing my phone up, I check my text messages.

Jackson: I have no idea what you are talking about.

I can almost hear the smile in his text.

Pushing the green phone icon at the top of the screen, I wait for Jackson to answer.

"I thought about letting it go to voicemail." His laughing voice comes through the phone.

The sound of his laughter is grinding on my already shot nerves.

"Why in the hell didn't you for one, tell me Ashlyn lived here in California and two, not only was going to school to be a firefighter, but somehow was ending up at my station?"

"Had a little of a surprise this morning, did you?"

"This isn't really funny."

"You're right, your tone is making it hilarious."

"Man, if I could punch you right now, not going to lie, I would."

"What are you so worked up about? According to you there was nothing going on between the two of you, so why would I have thought to tell you? You haven't mentioned her name even once the couple of times I have been out there, it's not like I'm just going to bring up the conversation, I just figured I would leave it alone."

He's right, I made sure I didn't mention Ashlyn when he came out to visit. I didn't want him thinking I was looking for more than just friendship with her.

"Seriously, man. No hey, my sister is going to be working with you, watch out for her. Or I don't know, a hey, Ashlyn moved to California, so if you get a call that she needs something, you know why. Nothing came to mind that you thought I needed to know about any of this?"

"There is no part of any of what you just said that I thought I would have had to ask you to do, man. Listen, you're my best friend and yes, when you told me you kissed Ashlyn I might have taken a few days to wrap my head around it, but in the long run, I've always known she had a crush on you and I would never have been mad if you two ended up together, I would have just kicked your ass if you broke her heart, which just for the record, you are lucky I didn't do before now."

Running my hands through my hair, I realize I'm not upset about Ashlyn's career choice or that she ended up here at my station, but more over that I had no idea any of this was happening.

The building vibrates as the tones go off, notifying us of yet another call this morning. "Hey, man, I have to go."

"Hey, Kayson."

"Yeah."

"In all seriousness, watch out for her."

Knowing what I say next makes everything I just complained about completely obsolete, I admit, "You know you never have to ask that. I'll make sure she is safe."

With that I hang up, run down the hall and out to the bay before the engine takes off without me.

Jumping up into the cab, Ashlyn is there, looking as calm as can be, that is to those who don't know her. I've known this woman most of her life and I'm seeing right past her tough exterior. It's the slightest of movement and if you weren't watching her closely you wouldn't see it, but she is chewing on the inside of her cheek and when I look down at her hands, she is rubbing the material at the side of her leg with her pinky. To top everything off, she is looking everywhere but at me, because she knows I'm seeing right through her.

I fist my hands to keep from reaching out and grabbing her hand just to reassure her that it's all good. However, if she is going to make it as a firefighter, I can't be holding her hand.

As much as she looks like a grown woman right now, I can't help but see that little girl in ponytails following us everywhere, or that girl who tried so hard not to cry the day her brother and I left for bootcamp, but at the end just before we turned to leave, she jumped into both our arms and made us promise to come home. Or the girl on her graduation, the excitement in her eyes when she opened her bedroom door to find Jackson and myself home a week early just to surprise her.

There was a time, before I went and ruined it all, when she would have been the first to call me and tell me that she was moving or that she had decided to become a firefighter.

"Murphy, Walker, most important thing to remember is that there aren't any heroes here, we are a team and we work as one. Pay attention to orders and watch out for

your fellow firefighter and everyone gets to go home."
Cap's voice comes through our headset.

I don't miss the look the new guy gives Ashlyn, it's a reassuring gesture that they've got this. Her smile that she gives him back doesn't go unnoticed either. Both actions grind on my nerves and I have to hold back the urge to side punch the guy in the arm. I remember when she used to look at me for reassurance.

CHAPTER

Eight

ASHLYN

FIRST CALL and it's a multiple car accident on the freeway. In morning traffic, this is something I'm sure this area sees a lot of. Everyone rushing around to get to work, calls are being made, makeup applied, everything to distract a driver and it takes seconds for something like this to happen.

When the bells go off at the station my heart jumps in my chest. My first call and I haven't been at the station for more than maybe an hour. I was warned about how busy this station was, but the guys had just rolled in from an earlier call and were now right back at it.

Grabbing my equipment from my locker, my body goes into robot mode and I do what I've been trained to do, but my mind is running a hundred plus. The captain instructs Neil and me to hop into the engine with him.

Settling into my seat, I'm trying everything I can to keep from showing how nervous I am.

Another firefighter jumps into the seat across from me and sticks out his hand. "We haven't been introduced yet, I'm Caleb but everyone calls me Striker."

Shaking his hand, I give him a puzzled look. "Striker, it's nice to meet you. Is there a good story behind that name?"

"It's followed me my entire life. Baseball pitcher in school, I was known for striking everyone out. In college everyone thought I would go pro, even got an offer, but decided I wanted to do something else, so I became a firefighter." He shrugs his shoulders like giving up the pros is no big deal.

I'm about to respond when Kayson jumps into the empty seat. I watch as he settles in, realizing that my heart still jumps in my chest the way it always did when I was a teenager.

As he settles into the seat, I look away so that he doesn't catch me staring at him and decide to concentrate on anything but him, mostly keeping from showing everyone how nervous I am.

As hard as I try to pay attention to the conversation between Striker and Neil, I can feel Kayson's eyes on me and it is so incredibly hard to keep my eyes from seeking his out.

I could have sworn the last three years had taken care of any stupid little girl, teenage girl, whatever you want to call it, crush I had on Kayson. However, watching him stalk up to me today, in uniform, did something to my insides that I haven't been able to settle and that feeling I had when he kissed me came slamming back at me.

I don't want to like him, I don't want to want him. If I would have known this was his station I would have maybe tried to trade. Nope, that's a lie, I would have decided to face off with him just to prove to myself I was over him, and how wrong I would have been.

When we were back at the station in that room and his lips were only inches from mine, it took everything I had not to close that space between us and kiss him, but he hurt me and I had my first heartbreak from the one guy I had loved since I could remember. It took me a little time to get over him kissing me and then leaving, but him not talking to me since, I think that's what hurt the most. Yes, he broke my heart, but him not talking to me since then I think has hurt a lot more.

Not one phone call, text or even Jackson mentioning he had asked about me, nothing. Even though my heart was crushed a little from him not feeling the same for me that I did him, it was more crushed over the friendship I thought we had but obviously didn't.

I was never more thankful for the captain's voice to come through our headsets and interrupt my train of thought. Now isn't the time to think about all of this, it's time to work.

Rolling up on scene, I stare out the side window and realize, no matter how much you prepare yourself for what this job may throw at you or the stories you hear and tell yourself you can handle, nothing can really prepare you for what you really deal with, especially your first call.

I'm the last to exit the cab, and as I hop down, Kayson is suddenly standing in front of me. "I'm right here if you need me."

He is looking at me like he used to, like a little girl, or his best friend's little sister, not the woman or firefighter I've become.

Rolling my eyes, I move my way past him, but before I walk away I look over my shoulder. "Too late for that."

I don't care how he takes my words or what he thinks I mean by them.

IT'S after one in the afternoon when we roll back into the station. After putting my stuff away, I sit on the bench and take a moment to take in everything that has happened today. I'm already exhausted and I've only been on one call.

Kayson, his name should mean exhaustion. This morning he charges me like a rhino and looks like he is about to rip Neil's head off. In the room earlier I would have sworn he was going to kiss me, and then throughout this entire call we just returned from, every time I turned he was right there. I don't want unneeded attention here, so I'm going to have to have a talk with Kayson, what I'm going to say I have no idea yet, but I'm here to do a job and that's it.

My phone vibrates in my pocket, pulling it out I see my brother's picture on the screen.

Pushing the little green circle under his picture, I answer, "Hey, Jackson."

"So how is everything going? Been on any calls yet? Meet anyone interesting at work? Have you made friends?"

There is laughter in my brother's voice and I realize he knew this whole time. "When did you know?"

"When you told me the station number, I realized it."

"And you didn't think I needed to know this little bit of information?"

"Would it have changed anything?"

I throw up my hand, like he could see me or something, "Yes, for one I would have been a little more prepared for the pissed off Kayson who stormed at me this morning and made a scene in front of everyone."

"He didn't."

My brother is laughing!

"This isn't funny, Jackson."

"It kind of is."

"I'm hanging up now."

Before he can reply, I push the end button and hang up on him.

My phone screen goes back to the home screen and I look down at the picture. It's from my graduation day, I'm in my cap and gown and both Jackson and Kayson are in uniform. They both surprised me that day by coming home a week early to be there for my graduation. This is my favorite picture. Even though it's been three years since I've seen Kayson, until today that is, I couldn't switch out the picture.

Footsteps coming up behind me has me quickly shoving my phone back into my pocket and turning to see who it is, hoping that it isn't Kayson.

Relief washes over me and my shoulders slump a little when I see one of the other firefighters grabbing something from his locker.

He looks over at me and smiles. I'm not sure which one he is, we haven't been introduced yet.

"Hi, I'm Ashlyn." I give him a slight wave.

"I'm Jeff, it's nice to meet you."

"You, too."

"Lunch has been laid out up in the kitchen, should probably grab something before we get called out again."

I take a deep breath, "They weren't kidding, this station is busy."

Jeff shrugs, "It can be, we have just learned to make the most out of mealtime when we can."

"Got it."

"Welcome to the crew."

I give him a small smile, "Thank you."

WALKING UP THE STAIRS, everyone is seated at the large table, passing around lunch meat, making sandwiches, and what looks to be a potato salad.

There is an empty seat between Neil and one of our engineers that I haven't learned the name of yet, but looking at his name tag I read Garrett Scott, and right across from that empty seat is Kayson.

Taking the seat, Neil right away hands me the bread and a platter of lunch meats with a smile. When I look over at Kayson he is glaring at Neil. All right, enough is enough. Hoping I land the mark I'm aiming for, I swing my booted foot under the table.

Kayson's eyes flash over to me, the only indication that my kick landed exactly where I wanted it to. I give him a slight shake of my head, silently telling him to knock it off.

His eyes bounce between me and Neil in a silent question. Rolling mine at him, I take a deep breath and look away, only to see that we have gained the attention of most of the table.

I can't do this anymore. The quiet stares from my coworkers that have been happening all day, and Kayson acting like an ass. It's time to just lay it out there for everyone, get the questions out of the way and maybe get Kayson to back off a little.

Taking a deep breath, I begin. "All right, so as some of you, or probably all of you have noticed, Kayson and I know each other outside of the station. I've known him since I was probably about four years old, he is my brother's best friend. The same brother thought it would be funny not to inform either of us on the fact that we would be working together and created a little bit of a shock, so please excuse any glaring from Mr. Shaw, he obviously doesn't take surprises very well. As for me, I'm excited to be part of this station and working alongside all of you, just ignore Kayson while he sulks."

The table erupts in laughter, and quickly the attention is brought back to the food on the table and not myself and the not-so-happy Kayson.

That's fine, he can be mad, he can send me all the warnings through his eyes that he would like, but from now on, I'm worrying about me. I'm here and he is going to have to deal with it.

CHAPTER
Nine

KAYSON

AFTER ASHLYN'S little announcement her whole attitude changed. She is smiling and laughing with the guys. As I watch the crew interact and her with them, I realize how much I've missed being around her the last few years. Not to mention, I was only home for a couple days after returning from the military and gone two years before that.

In those five years Ashlyn has gone from a teenager to the woman she is today. Before the day that Jackson and I got home I never looked at Ashlyn as anything other than my best friend's little sister, but when she opened her bedroom door and jumped into my arms the day of her high school graduation, something changed.

That's the night I kissed her and realization slammed into my chest that I was no longer thinking of her as my best friend's little sister, but a woman that I wanted. I knew that wasn't fair, our timing was all off. I was moving here to California. That put four states between us, not ideal for any kind of relationship, let alone one that had only contained one kiss.

Here she is again, thrust into my life and if anything, my need for her has only grown with time. However, she has made it very clear that she is here to work and seems content on forgetting anything that may have happened in the past between the two of us.

With each laughter of hers that fills the room and knowing that it's the guys in the station making her laugh, more so the new guy, it twists me up with a need that I thought couldn't get any tighter than it had. Never thought the one girl I'd want but couldn't have would be my best friend's sister.

After only a couple of bites of my sandwich and a scoop of potato salad I haven't touched, as well as listening to the conversations around the table, I need some air. Grabbing my plate, I push myself back from the table, make my way to the kitchen, throw away my unwanted lunch and head down to the bay. I need a little space.

GRABBING A RAG, I begin wiping down the engine, it's just busy work to try and keep my mind off Ashlyn. It's not working. This is insane. Throwing the rag against the wall, I plop down onto the bumper at the back of the engine and take a deep, frustrated breath. I run my hands through my hair, my elbows resting on my knees and my hands at the back of my neck.

"I didn't know you were here at this station, but if I had, I would have never guessed you would have a problem with me being here."

Her voice comes from my right, but I keep my eyes looking down. "I have no problem with you being here, Ash."

"You mean you are in this kind of mood all of the time? Must be making a ton of friends."

Letting my hands fall, I take another deep breath. We need to have this conversation. She isn't going anywhere, I'm not going anywhere, and in order for this job to be done right we need to be able to work together, so the only way to do that is to clear the air.

Standing up, I turn and face her and my breath lodges for a moment in my chest. In this uniform, her hair pulled back in a ponytail, as simple as it all is, she is stunning.

She has always been beautiful, but now she has sexy mixed with it.

"Why didn't you call me or something and let me know you were living here?"

"Kayson, the last time we talked, you basically told me you didn't want me and that you were moving here to California. You didn't call, you didn't text, we have already had this conversation today. I get that things were a little different because we kissed, but I never thought in a million years you would just cut all ties with me. I was young and yes, had a huge crush on you, but I wasn't so desperate as to bother you with calls or send texts that you were just going to ignore. Yes, I was heartbroken, but not desperate."

"I wouldn't have ignored you, Ash."

"The phone works both ways, Kayson, plus I have more respect for myself than to beg you to give us a chance. You didn't want me."

"It had nothing to do with not wanting you." My voice begins to rise, "You'd literally just graduated high school, I was moving four states away, what was I supposed to do?"

"You shouldn't have kissed me to begin with then," she throws back at me.

Our voices are starting to echo throughout the station and this isn't a conversation I want the whole station a part of.

Grabbing her hand, I'm surprised when she freely follows me as I lead the two of us out the side door to the side of the building. The whole station is gated in with the exception of the roll-up doors for the garage, so we don't have to worry about anyone else right now.

Once outside, I release her hand and pick up from where we left off inside.

"I'm not going to lie to you and say that I regret kissing you, or that I wouldn't do it again if I could go back. I was leaving, Ash, there was nothing I could do about it. Your life was just beginning. You had college and your own future to start working toward."

"That would have been for me to choose, not you, plus look where I ended up."

I don't know what to say next. She isn't going to see why I left the way I did.

"You know, every time Jackson came here to California to visit, I knew you two were hanging out, he would call me every night. Of course we got together, but never once did he invite me to hang out with you guys. I just assumed that was because you didn't want to see me. I think that's what hurt more than anything, Kayson. You have always been such a large part of my life and because of one kiss, you ended it all. You are right, I didn't tell you I was here, I honestly didn't think you would care."

Looking into her eyes, I see them starting to glass over and that's my undoing. Closing the space between us, I back her up against the wall and hold her there with my body. Her hands are on my chest and I'm waiting for her to try and push me away, but instead she fists my shirt in each of her hands.

"I'm not going to lie to you and tell you I didn't look at you as a sister for most of your life, but when you opened the door and threw yourself into my arms that day of your graduation, something shifted inside. I was seeing you for the first time as the woman you were becoming, not just Jackson's little sister that has followed us around most of her life. Kissing you that night, I was only taught one thing, it was going to be harder than hell to walk away from you, but I had to, for both our sakes."

Her eyes search mine and being this close I can no longer hold myself back. Closing the remaining space, I claim her lips with mine. It's not an apologetic kiss, it's the frustration of today, the need I've had for her for the past three years. It's desire, all wrapped in one.

For a moment she surrenders to it and I feel her kissing me back. A small moan escapes into the air around us, but I honestly have no idea from which of us it came.

Her hands tangled in my shirt tighten and pull at my shirt, I grab her ponytail and pull slightly, her small gasp allows just enough space for my tongue to find hers. How did I ever walk away from this woman?

Timing is everything at this station, the tones sound off all around the station and Ashlyn goes still in my arms. I start to push back to look at her, but her hands that were fisted in my shirt are now flat against my chest and she is pushing me back. Her eyes will not meet mine.

"Ash?" I take a step away from her.

She won't look at me, her fingers are now tracing her own lips and her breathing is labored. Without another word, she pulls the door open and disappears back inside.

The bells going off and the voice coming through our intercoms is a reminder that I need to put what just happened to the side for right now, it's time to work.

CHAPTER
Ten

ASHLYN

AS I GRAB my gear from my locker, I have to stop for a moment when I lose my balance as I try to quickly remove my shoes and step into my boots and turnout pants.

Taking a couple of deep breaths, I clear my head and lecture myself—now isn't the time. I can't be distracted like this on a call. Damn Kayson, what was he thinking? More so, what was I thinking for allowing it to happen?

Pulling myself together, I make it to the engine at the same time Kayson does, he steps aside for me to jump in first and then follows me up into the cab.

Neil and Cowboy are with us, both bouncing their questioning looks between myself and Kayson. I'm pretty sure everyone in the station heard the early part of our conversation and I swear my cheeks have permanently been a shade of red today. What a first day on the job.

"Shaw, Murphy, when we get back I would like a word with both of you," the captain's voice comes over our headset.

Great, two more shades of red just brightened my face, I'm sure. Everyone from the crew can hear this conversation.

"Yes, sir." I can hear my own voice through the headset as I respond to the captain and I hate how defeated it sounds.

I stare out the window so that I don't have to make eye contact with anyone. I just listen to the sirens and watch the city fly by.

Today was supposed to be the best day. Last night I got very little sleep, I was too excited. I had to have checked my bag twenty times to make sure I had everything. I sat there on my bed and stared at my uniform draped over my chair for probably an hour, so excited to put it on for the first time. I'm not delusional, I know this job is going to be trying and there are going to be things I wish I didn't have to see, but it can be so rewarding as well. I just want to do something that helps others.

Saddest part about today, it's not the job that is making it hard, it's Kayson. Out of all the damn stations in this city, how did this work out?

Pressing my lips together, I can still feel his on mine. The way his body felt pressed to mine, the sensation that zipped throughout my body when he pulled my hair to get to the place he wanted to be.

I've been on a few dates, was serious with one guy last year for about seven months, until I found out he thought I was wasting my time on my career path and would never make it. It didn't take me long to tell him goodbye. None of those before today have made me feel even an ounce of what Kayson made me feel just now outside of the station with a single kiss.

Something nudges my booted foot and I look over to see Neil watching me with a questioning look in his eyes.

He's a nice guy, but how tentative he is doesn't go unnoticed. I'm not one of those that thinks all the guys fall for me, but I'm getting the feeling that Neil may have a little something for me going on, it's hard not to see it.

I give him a slight smile and a nod and then turn my attention back to the window. I need to make sure I don't do anything to encourage him.

Rolling up to the house we were called out to, we are attending to a guy who was on the roof and decided to challenge gravity. He didn't win that battle, but was lucky that when he fell it was into a kid's blow-up pool, which probably helped cushion his fall enough to not sustain major injuries.

Most of the time we are there tending to the man's injuries, he and his wife are arguing. Him telling us that he told her not to call us out, that he was fine, her yelling back and the kids just watching. I actually make that my job. They have two little ones, I decide to keep them occupied while the parents argue and the guys go about checking the man for injuries.

It all distracts me enough that I'm feeling better, until we get back to the station that is.

As soon as I hop out and grab my stuff the captain is right there, "Don't forget I would like a word, please."

Nodding, I leave my stuff where it is and follow the captain and Kayson to the back of the building, out the door there and into the lot where we keep all our cars parked.

"Sir, I'm really sorry…" Captain puts his hand up to stop me before I can say much.

"Look, I'm not out here to lecture the both of you, but I'm going to suggest that whatever is going on between the two of you, may it have been in the past or now, you two figure it out and start working together. Ashlyn, you were highly recommended to us and Kayson, you have always been an amazing firefighter, I expect both of you while you are here at the station to keep things professional and work as a team. What happens between the two of you on your days off is between you guys, but here it's not important. I can't have the two of you distracted and…" he looks squarely at me, "I don't want to have you switched to another station."

"It was never my intention to cause a problem here and I can promise you it will not be an issue," I speak first.

"I didn't say you were causing problems, Murphy. It's my job to spot situations early and keep them from happening, that's what I'm doing here."

He doesn't even wait for us to respond, he turns and leaves the two of us alone.

I'm exhausted, and on the way back from the call the captain announced the two newbies, as he called us, were in charge of dinner tonight.

"Ash…"

I stop him before he can go on, "Look, this is ridiculous. What happened was in the past, I'm over it and have moved on. I've missed you, Kayson, I'm not going to lie, and I want to go back to having you as a friend."

"A friend? What about earlier?"

He is referring to the kiss and as much as I want to be in those arms, I know it's not a good idea.

"That shouldn't have happened."

"But it did."

He takes a step closer to me and I take a step back, holding up my hands to stop him.

"Kayson, please." I hate that my voice drips with pleading.

He doesn't move toward me, but he does watch me for a moment. I can't help but notice something has changed in him, but I don't want to argue with him anymore.

When he doesn't say anything, I turn and walk back into the station and back to where I left all my gear just sitting.

My phone vibrates in my pocket. Pulling it out, I see I have missed a few text messages, but the one I open is from Hannah.

Hannah: So, how is today going?"

Right now I would love nothing more than to have my best friend here, but she is back home and I can't talk, I have dinner for ten people to help make.

Me: Very unexpected is the best way I can describe it, but can't talk. Will call you later tonight or tomorrow when I get off work.

Hannah: Can't wait. Please stay safe.

Me: Promise.

Tucking my phone into by back pocket, I take a second to collect myself and then put on a very fake, but I'm hoping convincing smile. All I have to do is get through dinner with everyone. Try to keep the conversation and attention off Kayson and myself, of course that may be easier said than done, then hopefully be convincing that with an eventful first day I can turn in early, then just pray the night is quiet.

The answer to that wishful thinking are the tones going off throughout the station yet again. The rate this is going, I'm starting to wonder if dinner will even get made. Back to the engine it is.

CHAPTER
Eleven

KAYSON

GOING BACK TO BEING FRIENDS. That's what Ashlyn said. There was no going back after the first time I kissed her, and definitely not after the kiss today.

Before today, hell, even if you would have asked me before eight o'clock this morning what my feelings were for Ashlyn, I would have told anyone that even though I missed her, I was doing what was best for her.

I didn't reach out after I left because I knew that would make things difficult, I have to admit that would have been my lame excuse to keep from telling anyone that I was having a really hard time staying away. That's why I didn't return home much, instead I had Jackson come out here to California, less possibilities of running into her, not knowing she was right here all along.

Today, having her in my arms only confirmed that's where she belongs. It felt right. Her lips responded to mine with as much need as mine demanded from hers.

The smart thing to do would be to agree with her and the two of us to skate around this need for each other we have and just do our jobs and keep things on the friendship level, but every time I see the new kid hit on her, or one of the guys flirting with her, I want to grab her and show all of them she is mine. A little caveman I know, but that's what she does to me.

For the rest of shift I'm going to let it go. We don't need any more attention from the crew or the captain on this and I can tell Ashlyn is about done. Tomorrow we are both off and before we leave the station maybe I can convince her to go get breakfast with me or something and we can talk, clear the air between us a little. Maybe I can convince her why I walked away and decided not to reach out afterwards. Convince her that I'm not going to walk away from her again.

Pulling out my phone from my pocket, I figure there should be another phone call I make. I not only have to convince Ashlyn, but out of respect for our long friendship, I better call Jackson. Not for his permission, Ashlyn is an adult, but I want to keep my friend as well as get the girl. I'm not going to hide my feelings for his sister from him.

Pulling up his name, I hit the call button, and the tones once again go off throughout the station.

"Damn it."

"What's wrong, Ashlyn all right?" I hear a slight panic in Jackson's voice when he answers.

"Yea, sorry, she's fine, but we just got another call. I'll have to call you back later."

"No problem, talk later." Jackson hangs up before I have a chance.

Grabbing my gear, I purposely jump into the ladder truck this time knowing that Ashlyn will be in the engine. We are all going to the same location, but I think she needs a little space and in such tight confinement I can feel the tension radiating off her as she tries to ignore that I'm there.

If I have any hope of convincing her of anything tomorrow, I need to give her a little breathing room for the rest of the day.

I grab the seat up front with Garrett, our engineer. Before I even shut the door, he turns to me.

"Please tell me you didn't run from that girl?"

Garrett is married and has his first child on the way, so I know his interest in this isn't because he is interested in Ashlyn.

"No one's business, man."

"You two kind of made it everyone's business. You know there are no secrets around this place, this station is too open, every conversation echoes through here."

Slamming the door shut, I busy myself with inputting the location to the call. That's when Jeff decides to pop his head around the corner.

"I'm with Garrett, I'm kind of hoping we all heard wrong. You don't run from a woman like that."

"She's my best friend's sister, she'd just graduated high school and I was leaving the next day to move here, putting four states in between us. I didn't run away from her."

I had to give them something, or this conversation would move throuhout both engines over the headsets and I needed to end it before that. Ashlyn didn't need to hear any part of it.

Jeff irritates me further when he just nods his head and is giving me a shit-eating grin as if saying "sure you did" and pulls back to buckle up in his seat.

PULLING UP TO THE ADDRESS, both engines are rolling up. The house's garage is engulfed in flames, but it looks like the Fourth of July is exploding all around it.

Hopping out of the engine, we all stand back and watch as the show goes on. One of the officers on site comes up and starts explaining the situation to the captain.

"Well, we have a bunch of illegal fireworks, and when I say a bunch, the owner has informed us that over three-fourths of the garage was filled, floor-to-ceiling, with boxes of all types of fireworks." The officer points to a crowd of people on the sidewalk. "The guy over there is the owner, he has some burns that need looking at."

"Do we know how it started?"

The officer nods, "We do and you won't believe it. So this garage used to be his workshop for cars, he was inside, tripped over something with a cigarette and dropped it when he fell. Landed on some old oil or something on the ground, he said it went up fast. He tried putting it out before it hit the boxes..." He points up to the sky as the fireworks continue to go off, "He didn't make it in time."

"For sure nothing else in there, ammo or propane tanks for example? We don't need any surprises," Cap asks.

"He has told us there is nothing other than the fireworks."

"All right, guys, let's fan out around the space and start dumping, make sure we wet the houses around this property to keep anything else from catching fire." Cap starts shouting orders over the loud sounds surrounding us.

"Officer, have houses in the area been evacuated?" the captain asks.

"Yes, the only house we didn't get an answer from was next door, no car in the driveway, we have to assume no one is home."

Going around to the side of the engine, I go to grab a hose when the ground shakes from a large explosion. Everyone ducks down as we wait.

"What the hell was that?"

Looking over, the whole side wall to the garage is blown out and fireworks are starting to shot straight out from the side, one shoots right into the neighbor's downstairs window, the flames filling the space immediately.

"Get water over there now!" the captain starts yelling orders.

"Sir, sir." A woman's voice comes up behind me.

"Ma'am, I need you to back up, please, this isn't safe."

"Sir, there is a deaf teenage girl who lives in that house, her mom usually works late. If they knocked she wouldn't have heard them."

CHAPTER

Twelve

ASHLYN

THE NOISE around us is insane. I will never look at fireworks the same I don't think. When the explosion from the garage goes off, the ground under our feet shakes and I don't think I've ever felt heat like that in my life.

I notice the woman as she runs up to Kayson and listen to what she is telling him.

When she mentions a deaf girl, I turn and start scanning the windows of the house that is now on fire. It's a two-story and that's when I spot her, second floor, second window to the back of the house on the right side.

Grabbing Kayson's arm, I point up to the window. "Look."

He turns and spots the girl right away. I never expected him to just take action and run right to the house.

"Shaw, what are you doing? Get back here!" the captain yells as Kayson runs past him.

"Sir, look." I point up to the window again where the young woman is waving her arms at us.

"Get me two hoses over on that house now. Cowboy, get over there and follow Shaw. The rest of you, soak that side of the garage and keep anymore fireworks from going off. Stay back, though, not sure what exploded and the owner obviously cannot be trusted with the right information."

Grabbing a hose with two others, I race toward the house that Kayson and Cowboy just ran into.

As quick as everything starts, it ends. We are able to contain the fire in the house to just the living room and Kayson and Cowboy bring the girl out without any injuries. The fireworks show finally stops and this is definitely a story to tell for my first day on the job.

What a day. First a man and a blow-up pool and now a fireworks show, what next?

AN HOUR AND A HALF LATER, we are all mopped up and finally heading back to the station. Just in time for Neil and me to hop into the kitchen and start on dinner while everyone else cleans up the engine and truck and gets everything ready for the next call.

As I'm finishing up the salad, Neil rests his hip against the counter next to me. "So, can I ask you a question?"

Giving him a sideways questioning glance, I say, "Sure."

"What's going on between you and Kayson?"

"Nothing, why?"

"That man hasn't stopped staring at you all day. I can't even tell you how many times I've gotten a death glare from him."

Taking the sliced tomatoes I've just finished cutting and tossing them in the bowl with the salad, I wipe my hands on a towel and turn my attention to Neil.

"I'm sorry about Kayson. Like I mentioned earlier, he has known me since I was a little girl, he is just a little overprotective, like big brother."

"Those are not looks a big brother gives, Ashlyn, trust me on this. We all heard the conversation you guys had earlier, at least parts of it, what happened?"

"Honestly, nothing. I was young, just graduated high school and had a little crush, it happens. Other than that, nothing has happened."

Neil isn't buying it. I can see it written all over his face.

"He was an idiot."

Smiling, I grab the bowl with the salad, "We better sit down and eat before another call comes through."

I don't want to be rude, but I don't really want to stand here and discuss Kayson and my relationship either.

Thankfully, he drops it and just follows me to the table with the plate of chicken we made and the mashed potatoes.

WE MAKE it through dinner without any calls and the conversation around the table stays light, and away from Kayson and me.

Now I'm sitting along in this room. All I wanted to do earlier was escape here and now that I'm here, alone because everyone else turned in, I feel antsy. It's almost ten, which means it's almost eleven for Hannah. Maybe she's still awake.

Grabbing my phone, I search for her contact information and open up a text.

Me: It's late, are you awake?

Her text is sent back immediately.

Hannah: Yes, call me.

Hitting the little green icon on the top, I don't have to wait long for her to answer.

"So how was it today?"

"Are you ready for this?"

"That bad?"

I know I sound exhausted, I can hear it in my own voice.

"Well, the first maybe ten minutes that I was here was great, after that all downhill."

"Ash, you are killing me here, what happened?"

"Kayson is what happened."

"What are you talking about? What does Kayson have to do with how your day went? I'm so confused right now. Did he call you or something?"

"Or something. He works here at the station I'm at."

"Are you serious?"

"He caused a big scene this morning, has been in a mood all day."

"Why would he be the one to cause the scene? He is the one who left."

"He says he's mad because no one told him I'm here in California. I guess Jackson never mentioned it to him."

Hannah starts laughing.

"What's so funny?"

"Did Jackson know you two were going to be working together?"

"Yep."

"That totally sounds like something Jackson would do. So what else happened, or did he just sulk the whole day?"

I wasn't sure if I should tell her about the kiss. Hannah was all for me moving here to California, she just thought I should have contacted Kayson myself. I thought that made me seem desperate or something. If he wanted anything to do with me, he knew how to get a hold of me.

Being my best friend, I always expect Hannah to be on my side, but when everything happened three years ago she was more the voice of reason and she was reasoning with Kayson. Don't get me wrong, she thought it was wrong to do, but she understood why he did it, and that it didn't mean he didn't like me, just knew something so far apart would never work out.

She did start siding with me more the longer time went and he never called, but she has always been for Kayson and me to be together.

"One other thing happened." She's my best friend, and I tell her everything.

"What?"

"He kissed me."

"Like on the cheek or like kissed, kissed you?"

It was definitely not on the cheek. My lips could still feel his. Every time I think about it, my body starts to hum.

"Not on the cheek."

"I knew it, and I've been telling you, he likes you."

"Not the point, Hannah."

"What's your point then? You have loved that man since I can remember, go with it."

Just like that, she wants me to just jump into a relationship with him. No questions asked, no reserve for how he hasn't spoken to me in a few years, her answer to this is just do it.

"We work together now."

"And…"

"And, that could be disastrous. Plus, he kissed me, never said he wanted anything more."

"Ash, I get it. You don't want your heart broken again, but neither of you are in the same place as you were three years ago. Well, actually I guess technically you are, but not the point, you know what I mean."

"Aren't best friends supposed to be on your side?"

"I am on your side. I'm telling you to go for the man you have been in love with since you were in junior high."

This conversation was supposed to settle my mind a little, but it is only making me think more and right now I'm exhausted.

"I'll think about it, after I get some sleep and clear my head a little. Love you and miss you. You need to come visit."

"How many of those firefighters that you work with are good looking?"

"I believe to be a firefighter the rules state you have to be good looking."

"Then I will be visiting very soon."

This is why I love this girl.

"Night, talk soon."

"Don't fight it too hard, I mean make him work for it a little, he deserves that, but have fun. Night." She hangs up before I can say anything else.

For the next hour, I just lie here in bed. As tired as I am, I'm not sleeping. Picking up my phone from the night-stand, I sigh when I see that it's only one o'clock.

I can't just lie here anymore, throwing my pants back on over my shorts I'm wearing, I head downstairs in my socks and walk around the bay a little, playing with nobs on the engines, straightening my locker, although nothing was wrong with it, anything I can think of to keep me busy and get the early morning hours to move a little faster.

Sitting on the sidestep of the engine, my elbows resting on my thighs and my hands holding up my head, I watch a little bug move around the floor.

I never hear footsteps or any sounds, so when a pair of sock-covered feet come into my view, I jump up from my seat and can't stop the small scream that escapes my throat.

"Kayson, what are you doing down here?"

Leaning over, I try to get my heart to calm down from beating out of my chest.

"What are you doing down here?"

Standing up straight again, I answer, "I couldn't sleep, lot on my mind. It's been one hell of a first day."

The corner of his mouth goes up into a shy little smile, I used to love that smile on him. My chest tightens and I realize the more I'm around him the more I have missed him.

"I'm sure I need to apologize for some of it."

His hands are tucked into his pockets and he keeps looking down at his socked feet.

"Well, the fireworks were fun." I try to lighten the mood a little.

I don't want to argue with him anymore. So maybe if we don't bring up what happened today and just move forward, we can actually work together.

"Ash, I need to apologize. For today, for three years ago. My intentions were never to hurt you and I know I did. I need you to know, though, it wasn't easy for me to leave. I have picked up my phone more times than I care to admit to and started to call you, or send a text, I just didn't think you wanted to hear from me."

"I'm not mad at you for leaving. Well, that's a little bit of a lie, you did hurt me a little when you left, but to be honest it was the silent treatment I've had a harder time with."

"You didn't call me."

He was right, I didn't. I didn't want to be one of those girls.

"I know. I'll be honest, I didn't know what to say. I knew my feelings for you were different than yours were for me. I'm just Jackson's little sister."

His movement is quick, he closes the space between us before I know what is happening. My back is pressed up against the door of the engine and his arm is around my waist, holding me tight to him.

"Before that night I kissed you, yes, you were Jackson's kid sister, but after I had a taste of these sweet lips, you were no longer that little girl. Walking away from you was one of the hardest things I've done. Staying away from you is even harder."

His lips are so close to mine they tickle my lips as he speaks. I should move, pull myself out of his arms, walk away. Tell him we can be friends and then go to bed, but no part of my body is obeying what my brain is thinking.

His eyes bounce between mine and my lips as though he is asking me permission, and I know I should be making the move to say no, but I can't and if I'm being honest with myself, I don't want to. I want him to kiss me. It's probably going to be a mistake, I am probably going to get hurt again, but right now none of that matters. What matters is how nice it feels to have his arms wrapped tight around me. I feel safe, like nothing in the world could harm me. His chest is strong against mine, pressed so tight against me I swear I can feel his heart beat against my own rapid one.

"I'm going to kiss you again, Ash." Before I can say anything back, his lips are hard against mine.

A small groan escapes from my chest and my arms wrap around his neck as one hand buries deep into the hair at the back of his head. I'm holding on tight, because I know at any minute my legs are going to give out from under me.

His tongue demands my lips part and plays along with mine. I've kissed guys, but none of those times did it feel like this. Kayson is in complete control, he is demanding what he wants and I am freely allowing him all access. Although I know if I pull away right now, he would let me. I can feel his need for me, the security in being with him. His arms feel like a safe haven and I don't want to leave their embrace.

All day I've been trying to convince myself that all that needs to be between the two of us is friendship. That would keep my heart safe and there wouldn't be any disappointments. Right now, I'm throwing all of that caution out and am willing to do whatever this man wants.

His lips part from mine and I hear my own small whimper of disapproval.

"Ash, I need to know that you forgive me." His voice is low, but I hear the pleading in it.

Our eyes connect and I stare into the deep blue depth. This is the man I have dreamt about being with since I can remember. Other relationships never worked out because I was comparing them to him.

These past few years without him being a part of my life was hard, but after today I'm not sure if we can go back to just being friends. So basically, I have to decide if I want to forgive him and take a chance on where this will go, or walk away from him altogether and just figure out a way to work with him.

"What do you want, Kayson?"

"I want the woman who has been in my dreams to finally be mine. I don't want to play games, Ash. I want all of you and I promise you will have all of me. I'm not going anywhere this time."

I took a chance with moving here to California. I took a chance in becoming a firefighter and both of those have worked out for me. This is the one thing I have wanted for so long, how can I not take a chance on this as well?

That slow, sexy smile he gets starts to spread across his face, and before I know it, his lips are crushing mine once again. His hands have worked their way under my t-shirt and the moment his skin touches mine, I swear lightning shoots throughout my entire body. My skin hums under his touch as though it's calling out for him to touch me everywhere.

He pushes up my shirt and sports bra that I'm wearing, but only far enough for my breasts to be exposed. With my shirt's position, my arms are bound over my head and I'm pinned to the engine, my body to do as he please with.

His lips leave mine, but his eyes stay locked with mine as I watch him lower his head to one tight, pleading nipple. His eyebrow arches up, silently asking me if what he is about to do is all right.

Arching my back, I beg him to take what he wants. His eyes still locked with mine, a sexy ass smile spreads across his lips right before his tongue slowly circles one very tight nipple.

My head falls back against the engine and I have to lock my knees so that I don't end up on the floor.

He takes my breast fully into his mouth and I have to press my lips together to keep from calling his name out.

Like cold water being dumped over my head, I realize where we are. I start frantically wiggling against him and trying to move away, but with my arms pinned I'm making much progress.

His eyes meet mine full of question.

"We are in the station, not the best location." I direct my eyes to the upstairs reminding him we aren't alone.

Kayson doesn't miss a beat, he pulls away from me, but not far, just enough to open the door to the cab of the engine, then he grabs me around the waist and lifts me up into the engine, quickly following behind me.

"This is your solution?"

"Sound doesn't travel in here like it does out there."

He lightly pushes me and I find myself falling back onto one of the seats, Kayson kneels down in front of me.

"I don't think this is a good idea."

His hands have already made their way under my shirt once again and he has pushed it up, cupping both of my breasts in his hands. My head falls back against the seat and just like that I don't care where we are, as long as his hands are on me.

"Eyes on me." His voice is husky.

My eyes land on his and he smiles. Using the strength in his legs only, he lifts himself up enough to capture one breast in his mouth.

My fingers dig into his scalp, pushing his head down to me, begging for more of what he is doing with his tongue around my nipple.

He continues to torture me with his mouth as his hands move to my shorts. I feel him beginning to pull them down over my hips. I slightly lift my hips to help him with the task he has at hand.

Clothing out of the way and now around my ankles, I almost want to hide my face imagining what a sight he must be looking at. My shorts around my ankles, my shirt and bra pushed just above my breasts, everything in between fully exposed to him.

His hands are back on my hips and I watch as he pulls them toward him in the seat, this causing my legs to spread for him.

I watch his eyes take me in and his tongue swipe over his lips. He leans forward, his eyes back on mine and I can't look away as I watch the lightest swipe of his tongue against my throbbing core.

My body jumps, and my breath catches in my throat. Then he repeats the motion again, only this time his tongue makes tiny circles on the tight bud and I'm doing everything I can not to scream out.

In this truck or not, if I let go of what I'm feeling, I'm waking up the whole station.

That's when something in the distance starts pounding in the back of my head, and before I know what's happening, Kayson is pushing away from me and working on pulling my clothes back in order.

My brain finally clears enough to realize the tones are going off in the station. Pushing away his hands, I start rearranging my own clothes and quickly follow him out of the engine before anyone comes down.

I reach my gear just as the crew starts running down the stairs.

My heart is pounding in my ears. I know my face is five shades of deep red and I'm just praying that everyone is not quite awake enough to realize what Kayson and I were doing down here.

CHAPTER
Thirteen

KAYSON

THESE DAMN TONES have really bad timing. I watch Ashlyn as I step into my turnouts and grab my gear. Her head is down and she is trying to step into her turnouts, but keeps fumbling with everything.

Pulling my suspenders up over my shoulders, I grab my jacket and make my way over to her, placing a hand under her elbow to help her balance. She pulls away from my touch as though it burns and when her eyes meet mine, they are a white blue and look glassed over, as though she is holding back tears.

Shoving her foot into her booted pant leg, she grabs the rest of her stuff and heads for the engine, ignoring me completely.

I'm not sure what just happened, but it's twisting me up inside to know that she is upset, again.

I didn't plan anything like what just happened tonight. I wasn't looking to talk to her until the morning.

I was lying in bed, listening to one of the guys, pretty sure it was Striker, shake the room with his snoring and wasn't able to sleep. My brain just wouldn't shut off.

When I came down and saw her sitting on the side of the engine looking like every memory I have of her, I couldn't turn and walk away. I didn't intend for things to go as far as they did, but once I had her lips, I needed more and she wasn't stopping me.

Now we are back to the silent treatment and ignoring me. I thought we had moved past this and she had forgiven me. Her reaction just now is saying the complete opposite.

I'm pretty sure none of the guys have any idea what we were doing down here, if they do they aren't showing it.

I pull myself up into the engine, sitting across from her. She already has a steady stare out the window.

I nudge the toe of her boot slightly with mine, but she only pulls her foot back farther away from mine.

With calls that we go out onto in the middle of the night, no one is very talkative. Most of us sway in our seats and try to stay awake, so I don't think the others with us in the engine have noticed anything off about her.

Rolling up to a restaurant fire, everyone seems to wake up a little as we each jump out of the engine. Cap starts with the orders and everyone works like robots. I make sure to keep myself close to Ashlyn, only because I know she isn't herself right now. She isn't showing it in outward signs. She is fighting just as hard as anyone else in the crew, but I see it in her stance, in the way she communicates. Everyone else may think she is fine, but I've known her longer and I know she isn't all right.

We don't arrive back at the station until around six. Our shift ends at eight, so most of us realize going back to bed is useless and just jump into showers and get our stuff ready to head home. Maybe find a recliner and pass out for a short time, but we are all ready to have this shift over.

Ashlyn went straight to her room when we got back and I haven't seen her come out. So like everyone else, I grab a quick shower, pack up my stuff and hope that another call doesn't come in before we are able to leave.

Eight o'clock sharp and as the next shift comes in to relieve us, we start filtering out. I still haven't seen Ashlyn. With everyone up and about, I don't want to go and knock on her door to talk, I just wait.

Throwing my gear into the back of my truck, I turn to see her coming out with her gear bag in hand.

Walking over, I make a move to grab it from her. She pulls it back and walks past me.

"Are we not talking again? I thought we cleared this all up last night?"

She continues her walk toward a four-door SUV. I stand there and watch as she opens the back, throws her bag in and then shuts the back hatch. She just stands there for a moment, her back to me, her shoulders slumped over.

"Hey, Ash…" I start to close the distance between the two of us, taking a couple steps in her direction.

She quickly turns on me, "No," and puts her hand out to stop me. Then she looks around to see if anyone else is out here.

"Ash, we need to talk about this."

"I know, but right now I need to go home and get some rest. I don't want to talk here, everyone is already too aware of us."

"Look, why don't you go home, get some rest and then let me take you out tonight. We can go have dinner and talk. Tomorrow we are back on shift and I think it's best if we clear all of this up before then."

Taking a deep breath, she nods, "All right, my number is still the same, do you still have it or did you delete it?"

"Of course, I have it. I've already told you, it wasn't like that. I'll text you a little later with what time I'm going to pick you up."

"Maybe we should just meet somewhere."

I walk over to the driver's side of her car and open the door and wait for her. "I'll be picking you up."

Rounding the car, she stops before she sits down into the driver's seat. "What's changed now?"

"Nothing has changed, Ash, I'm just no longer fighting it." Leaning forward, I kiss her lightly on the lips and then pull back before I give into the need to grab her and throw her in my truck and just take her home with me.

"I don't understand."

"Tonight, we'll talk. Go get some rest, it was a little bit of a crazy day yesterday."

"No thanks to you," she mumbles as she sits down into the seat.

Starting her car, I shut the door for her and stand back a little as she backs out of the spot and pulls out of the station's parking lot.

Pulling my phone from my pocket as I head over to my truck, there is one phone call I have to make before anything else happens between Ashlyn and myself.

Hitting the green circle, I open my truck door and step up into the driver's seat while I wait for Jackson to answer the phone.

"Hey, man, what's up?" Jackson answers after the third ring.

"Did I wake you?"

"Nope, just leaving for the gym actually."

"This won't take long, but I wanted to talk to you."

"Sure, what's up?"

I'm not going to beat around the bush and have idle conversation while I work up the nerve to tell him what's going on. I'm just going to come right out with it.

"Remember when I told you about kissing your sister and how it wasn't going to happen again?"

There is silence on the other end of the line. Running my hand through my hair, I'm realizing I could lose my best friend over this.

"Go on," his voice finally comes over the line.

"I lied. Before you say anything, let me explain. That night of her graduation when we kissed, something triggered in me and I'll admit, for the first time I was seeing her for the woman she had become, not just your little sister. However, I knew I was leaving for California and there was no way to make anything between the two of us work. I'm not going to lie to you, man, I haven't stopped thinking about her for the past few years. Then she ends up here yesterday and every time one of these guys looks at her, I want to punch them, then we kissed again. I can't walk away from her this time and as soon as I convince her that she can trust that I'm not going anywhere, I don't plan on letting her go, which I'm hoping I convince her of tonight when I take her out."

I wait for a moment and let the silence stretch between the line. "Jackson, you are my best friend, we have been through a ton together and I don't want to do anything to jeopardize our friendship. You are like a brother to me, but I can't ignore my feelings for your sister either and I'm hoping you understand."

A few more silent seconds pass and finally he responds. "I'm not sure what has taken you so long. I figured it out the first time I visited you. You have the picture of you and her up in your living room. Single guys don't usually put pictures out of women they are going to have to explain to other women. Ashlyn is an adult and if she is willing to give you another shot then I'm good with it, I know she is in good hands. On the flip side, though, know if you hurt her, the best-friend-like-brothers card isn't going to save you."

Laughing, I release the breath I just realized I was holding. "Fully understand, I would probably kick my own ass."

"So besides all the trouble I can only imagine you caused for her, how did she do out there?"

"Let's just put it this way, I wouldn't want to be on her bad side, she is strong and keeping up with each of us just fine. She's going to be a great firefighter."

"I know she talks tough and can keep up, but on a serious note, watch out for her, she's still my little sister."

"Like I said yesterday, you don't have to worry, I'm going to be right there and watching over her, but don't be surprised when she calls and tells you how she had to save my ass one day."

"Probably, that does sound more likely. Hey, man, I'm going to go and get to the gym before I have to head to work. Good luck tonight, you are going to need it. She's stubborn."

Stubborn doesn't even begin to explain Ashlyn. "All right, man, talk to you soon."

CHAPTER
Fourteen

ASHLYN

MY INTENTIONS WERE to come home, take a long bath and then sleep most of the day, but a certain man is not only ruining my days at work, but my days off as well.

Every time I close my eyes, I see him looking up at me as he was setting my body ablaze. Or the feel of him pressed tight against me as he has me pinned to the wall or even the engine, kissing me as though he's afraid if he lets go of his tight hold, I may just disappear. Then there was that gentle kiss, just to say goodbye.

I'm not mad at Kayson for what happened early this morning at the station. I'm more upset with myself because I keep forgetting everything around me when he is around. For a moment there I believed we could maybe have something between us, I melted into his words and his arms. I'm mad because as hard as I fought to make myself believe I was over him, yesterday, this morning, right now all proves how very wrong I was.

It's easy to believe you are over someone when you don't see them, talk to them, never hear their name mentioned. When he jumped out of that engine yesterday morning, wearing turnout pants, and looking like a man that just worked to save the world, my heart flipped in my chest and every feeling I've ever had for the man slapped me right back in the face.

If I was to give us a chance and for some unforeseen reason it didn't work out, what then? We work together, he's my brother's best friend and I would never keep him from my family, they're his family, too. This could all go very wrong.

That's why I'm upset. I hate that I want him...just not sure if I should have him.

A TEXT from Kayson dings on my phone around three.

Kayson: Are you still obsessed with pizza?

Me: Some things never change.

Kayson: Great. I know the perfect place. I'll pick you up around six. Need your address.

After messaging him my address, I scroll through my contacts until I get to Hannah's name. I know whose side she is on. I say his, but she tries to convince me that it's mine, because she knows we are perfect for each other.

One ring and she answers. "So, how did the first day end, since I already know how it started?"

"With us making out in the engine in the early morning hours, almost getting caught because of a call."

"Wait…what?!"

"You heard me, we made out in the engine."

"You mean after I talked to you last night, there was more?"

"When I say made out, let's put it this way, there isn't a part of my body he isn't familiar with."

Hannah's screech has me moving the phone away from my ear. "I knew it. Are you guys like a thing now?"

"No, but we are going out tonight for pizza. I'm still not sure this is a good idea."

"Why are you fighting this so hard?"

Looking over at the coffee table where I have the same picture as I have on my phone screensaver, the one of the three of us from graduation, my heart flips in my chest.

"Honestly, I'm afraid that if this doesn't work out, I'll lose him from my life altogether, maybe keeping it just friends, or me being the annoying little sister is a better idea. I'm not sure I'm willing to take the chance."

"Ash, you are never going to be looked at by Kayson as the annoying little sister anymore. The man has had the woman."

"Hannah…"

"What? You're the one who just told me about the make-out session, although I would say that was a little more than a make-out, but call it what you would like. I say go for it. I do have one question, though."

"What's that?"

"How good does that man look in the uniform?"

"There are no words to describe it."

A man's voice comes from the other end of the line and it stops me in my thoughts. It sounds very familiar. I hear Hannah's voice, but she must have her hand covering the mic because she is muted and I can't tell what she is saying. She hasn't mentioned seeing anyone. Although now that I think about it, it kind of sounded like Jackson's voice.

"Hey, I have to go."

"Are you seeing someone?"

"I'm at work, one of the waiters had a question."

Hannah is a manager at one of the restaurants back home while she finishes out her nursing school, so what she is saying makes sense.

"All right, love you. Talk soon."

"Ash, before I go. You need to go for it. It'll be worth it."

"Maybe. Bye." I hang up my phone and stare at it for a moment.

I know my best friend, something is off and that voice… I think I'm tired, and right now I need to get ready before Kayson shows up. Making a mental note to ask questions the next time I talk to her, I toss my phone onto the coffee table and head back to my room to get ready for my date.

Holy crap, I have a date with Kayson!

SIX O'CLOCK ON the dot the doorbell sounds throughout my little house.

Each step I take toward the door, the butterflies intensify in my stomach. I have no idea why I'm so nervous, it's Kayson, not some guy I haven't known my entire life.

Wiping my nervous hands on my pant legs, I open the door and am slammed with a sight that will forever be imbedded into my head.

Kayson is standing there in dark blue jeans and a black button-up shirt, the sleeves rolled up over his elbows. The black shirt and his dark hair surrounding those blue eyes have them brighter than I have ever seen them and right now they are looking at me like they did early this morning.

He holds out a gift bag to me. "I know you hate flowers, so I went a different route."

Taking the bag, I look inside and find three packs of Rolos, my favorite, and a bag cheddar & sour cream chips.

"You remembered."

"I told you, I've never forgotten."

Holding out his hand to me, I set the bag down on a table I have against the wall of the hallway and then take his offered hand.

"Come on, I'm starving."

THE PIZZA PLACE he picked is perfect. It's not all quiet and fancy, where you have to whisper if you don't want the whole restaurant to hear your conversation. It's very laid back and casual, more my style.

Kayson orders my favorite pizza. Pepperoni, Canadian bacon and bacon. I've never been big on vegetables. He also keeps the conversation between the two of us very light, asking about the fire academy, schooling and how I've liked living in California.

"So, are you going to tell me what made you decide to be a firefighter?"

Shrugging, I answer, "I like to help people."

"So you just woke up one morning and said, I want to be a firefighter? You could have been a nurse..."

"What are you saying? Being a woman, a nurse would have been a better suited job?"

"That's not what I'm saying at all. I'm not like that and you know it. You were handling yourself just fine yesterday. You just never mentioned that's what you were looking at doing."

"Kayson, you guys were gone for almost two years before you came home on my graduation day, and then left two days later. We didn't have much time to talk about my future, you were leaving to continue yours. It's not like we talked much after you left for you to know either."

"You're right. I'm sorry and I'll keep saying I'm sorry until you believe that my intentions weren't to hurt you, Ash."

Taking a deep breath, I sit back into the booth and stare at him for a moment. He is holding with one hand the glass with his beer and swirling it around. His eyes bounce between mine and the liquid twirling around.

"I'm the one who is sorry, Kayson. We have already hounded out this conversation a couple of times in the last day, I don't need to keep bringing it up. It's been a few years and both of us have grown since then, it needs to be left back then."

"So you are saying you forgive me?" His eyes look up from is glass and there is that smile again.

"Kayson, I haven't been holding a grudge, I moved past all of that back then. I was hurt, I'm not going to lie, you have been a large part of my life and one kiss changed all of that. Yesterday you were the one who stormed out of that engine with smoke coming out of your ears."

He leans over the table and takes my hand in his, "Ash, let me explain something to you. Three years ago, I kissed this girl." He points at me with his other hand as though I need confirming that girl was me. "That one kiss spun my head. When you opened your bedroom door and threw yourself into my arms earlier that day, something kicked in my gut, but I pushed it aside. The moment I claimed those lips, I wanted to grab you and not let go. Like I explained, I felt you needed to start your life, and mine was moving me here to California. In my head there was no way to make that work. Then yesterday morning, the girl that has been in my dreams every night since that kiss is standing with another man, in my station."

"You make it sound like I brought a man to work."

Kayson shrugs, "I had no idea what was going on, but thinking you were with someone else and not me sent me over the top. That's when I realized, three years ago, I made a huge mistake. I wasn't mad at you, I was furious with myself."

"I had only met Neil a couple of minutes before."

"I know that now, but when he stepped between us to protect you from me, I almost laid the guy out. Protecting you has always been mine and Jackson's job, I never thought there would be a day someone would think you needed to be protected from me. That just pissed me off more. Plus, it doesn't help the guy is interested in you."

Kayson's hand is tightening around mine. It doesn't hurt, but it's like he is making sure I don't pull away from him.

CHAPTER

Fifteen

KAYSON

I DECIDED today while I sat around and waited for the time to leave that I wasn't holding anything back from Ashlyn. Any question she asked I was going to answer honestly. I want her to know this isn't something I just decided I want. This is something I am going to fight for.

"Nothing is going on with me and Neil," she confirms.

"I know, but between the shock of seeing you standing in the station and all day long him being right there, I just lost it a little."

"A little?" She gives me a questioning look.

"All right, not my proudest moment. I'm sorry."

She laughs, "Maybe we should start fresh, put everything behind us and just start all over."

"What do you mean by start over?"

"I don't know. What do you want?"

There aren't any words that can describe to her what I want. Releasing her hand, I reach to my back pocket and pull out my wallet. The check hasn't been brought to our table yet, but I throw down enough money to cover the food and extra for the waitress.

Ashlyn is watching me with questions in her eyes. Standing up, I reach for her hand. She places her hand in mine and I pull her up from her seat.

"What are we doing?"

"It's time to leave."

I lead her out of the restaurant, informing the waitress as we pass her that I have left payment on the table.

We cross the parking lot to my truck, when we reach the passenger side, I place my free hand on her waist and push her up against my truck.

Her eyes round with shock. Taking her hand that I'm holding, I place it on my chest right above my heart.

"Do you want to know what I want, Ashlyn?"

Her eyes are bouncing between mine, my lips and where her hand is at on my chest. "Yes, Kayson, I want to know what you want."

"I want you to understand, that pounding you feel under your hand, that's the way my heart beats every time I'm around you. I want you to know, it's yours and has been yours. I don't want to start over, I want to start where we left off, three years ago that night that I first kissed you and early this morning. I want you."

Before she can say anything in return, I bring my hand up over her neck, burying my fingers into the hair behind her ear and claim her lips. I feel her hand fist my shirt as her other one comes up over my shoulder and she pulls me tight to her.

My lips trail from her mouth to her neck.

"Kayson, we are in a very public parking lot."

I bring my eyes up to hers, pressing my forehead to hers as we both catch our breath. She's right, this isn't the place.

Once I've caught my breath, I grab the passenger door handle and open the door, stepping back as I open it to allow her to get in.

She smiles shyly as she looks around and then hops up into her seat. Shutting the door, I round the front and she has reached across and opened my door for me by the time I reach for it.

Nothing is said between us as I drive us back to her house. Parking alongside the curb, I throw the truck in park and turn off the ignition.

I look over at her, but her eyes are looking out the passenger window toward her house.

I unbuckle my seatbelt then reach over and unbuckle hers. This brings her attention to me. I'm about to ask her what's going through her mind when she surprises the hell out of me by turning her body to me, reaching across, grabbing the front of my shirt and pulling me to her. Our lips crash together, the center console of my truck keeping me from pulling her into my lap.

Pulling away, I ask, "Can I come in?"

She doesn't even think about it, she just nods her head. Pushing my door open, I jump down, shutting the door as I quickly make my way to the passenger side. Opening the door, she instantly leans over, wraps her arms around my neck and pulls my lips back to hers, then wraps her legs around my waist.

With one hand I support her weight under her legs and butt, the other I reach around and shut the door, and begin the walk, carrying her up to her door.

She starts laughing against my mouth.

When we reach the door, she drops her legs and slides down my body. Grabbing her keys out of her purse, she opens the door and I follow her into the hallway. Making sure to shut the door behind me, I realize there is no reason to hold back now. I've been wanting her since I tasted her earlier, tonight I'm going to have all of her.

She begins to walk down the little entryway, but I grab her hand and bring her to me, wrapping my arms around her and claiming her lips. My tongue instantly finds hers. Her chest vibrates against mine as a small moan escapes. That little moan alone could drop me to my knees and have me begging for her.

I need to slow us down just a little. Ending the kiss, she whimpers a little when I take a step back.

"Ashlyn, you're mine."

"I've always been yours, Kayson."

Picking her up, I ask, "Where's your room?"

She points straight down a small hallway and I make very short time getting us to it.

Walking straight over to the bed, I set her down onto her feet. As much as I would love to take it slow, worship each part of her body and show her what she does to me, I can't wait any longer to have her body, naked, wrapped around mine.

CHAPTER
Sixteen

ASHLYN

MY FEET TOUCH the ground and I have to fight the need to wrap myself around his body and crawl back up into his arms.

His eyes are staring straight into mine. They look like a white-blue flame and the intensity in them has me burning up inside.

Kicking off my shoes, I raise my arms above my head and wait. There's that cocky grin he gets that sets my core on fire.

Kayson takes one very small step toward me to fill in the space between us, his hands go to the hem of my shirt and slowly raises it over my stomach, chest, his fingers lightly brushing against my skin as he moves it up my body. Pulling it up and over my arms, he lets it drop to the floor. His fingers make a trail as they come back down, his lips now on my neck, kissing his way over to my shoulder where I feel his teeth bite down lightly.

Bringing my arms down, I find the buttons of the front of his shirt and quickly make work of them, then slide his shirt down over his arms and let it fall to the floor next to my discarded shirt. I allow myself a little time to appreciate the muscles along his arms as they flex under my touch. I can't wait to have them wrapped around me and feel all that strength holding me.

I make my way over his shoulders, down his chest, feel the definition of muscle over his stomach and stop at the top of his jeans. I make short work of his belt, button and zipper on his jeans, feeling his hardness as my fingers unzip his pants.

This morning he was all in control and took what he wanted, now it's my turn. Grabbing each side of the waist of this jeans along with the waistband of his boxer briefs, I push them down his legs, dropping to my knees in front of him as I go.

Wrapping a hand around the base of his hardness, I hear a sharp intake of breath from Kayson. Looking up, his eyes are closed and his hand is on the mattress of the bed, I believe helping him from losing his balance.

"I want your eyes." I repeat the same thing he told me in the engine.

His eyes open and I watch as they turn a bright blue color as I lean forward and slowly take him into my mouth. My name falls from his lips, his hand is now on the top of my head holding me to him.

I slowly pull back, sucking hard and allowing my tongue to cradle the under side of is hardness as I go. Then just as slowly I bring his full length back into my mouth, repeating it a couple of times, a little faster each time.

Kayson reaches down, grabbing me by the upper arms and bringing me back up to my feet. His hand reaches around my back, quickly unclasping my bra and it joins the clothes already making a pile on the floor. I watch as he quickly steps out of his shoes and removes his pants completely.

I take a moment to enjoy the full view of this man. Watch as each muscle flexes. The rest of my clothing is removed quickly and when I want nothing more than to wrap myself around his very inviting strength, he turns me toward the bed, and pushes me over so that my chest and stomach are flat on the mattress, my backside to him.

He leans over me and whispers in my ear, "I need to be inside of you."

I nod and I feel one foot sliding mine apart. I gasp a little when I feel him starting to enter me from behind. I press myself back against him, begging him for more. His hands are on my hips, mine are fisted in the comforter of my bed.

He pulls out slowly and then thrusts his hips to mine, pushing himself even deeper into me. My back arches, begging for more and he repeats his movement. Each time a little faster and a little deeper.

His name escapes my lips, but is muffled by the comforter I'm pressed into. Just as I think I'm about to fall apart, he pulls out.

I'm about to protest, when he stands me back up and turns me around. He picks me up, my legs wrapping around his waist, him guiding himself back into my very wet heat. He sits down on the edge of the bed and his hands go to hips once again. Slowly he pushes me back and then pulls me back to him. My head falls back at this new position, as he is hitting the very sensitive bud that has been begging for some attention. My back arches, pushing my breasts at him.

When his mouth sucks my breast fully into it, my head flies up and our eyes lock. His teeth nip at the very tight nipple. Between that and the rhythm we have moving between us, and the look in his eyes as he holds mine, daring me to look away, I can't hold onto my release any longer.

His hands guide me one last time hard onto him, he sucks hard onto my breast and I'm gone. My arms wrap tightly around his shoulders as I hold on as the world around me rocks. I can feel with each pulse of my release my body bringing him deeper and deeper into me and that just makes my release that much stronger.

I hear my name against my chest as his arms wrap tightly around me and his body goes stiff as he finds his release as well.

I'm completely wrapped around Kayson and we sit here for a moment as we both try to catch our breath.

After a moment, I start to slide back to untangle ourselves from each other. His hands are on my hips, keeping me from falling to the ground.

Once I've moved myself to the bed, I pull back the covers and slide myself against the welcoming cool sheets.

Kayson stretches himself out along side of me, wrapping his arms around me as he goes and pulls me tight to him. Part of me wants to protest because the cool sheets feel amazing against my heated skin, but then being wrapped up in Kayson's strength and being held by him, hot or not, is a more amazing feeling.

His hands begin to wander over my hips and backside. "I don't think I've had enough of you yet."

Stretching my neck back I go to respond, but he takes my lips before I can say anything. He moves us until I'm under him.

He kisses a trail down my neck where he nestles for a moment, his hand has come up and cupped one of my breasts, his finger and thumb doing something wickedly amazing to my very tight nipple.

Arching my back, I beg him silently for more.

Reaching down, I wrap my hand around his hardness and guide him to my already throbbing core.

"So greedy." He looks up at me with a smile before he takes a breast into his mouth and sucks hard.

His name fills the room as I beg him for more.

His body over mine, he adjusts his hips and I guide him to where my body is begging the most for him. He sinks down deep into me and I sigh with content.

His lips move back to mine as his hips begin to find their rhythm. Slow at first, but I wrap my legs up around his waist and thrust into him each time he thrusts his hips into mine, driving him deeper and deeper each time.

His forehead is pressed to mine and our eyes are locked as together, for the second time tonight, we find our release.

My legs fall from around his waist, but he doesn't move from his position on top of me. He just stares down into my eyes. I think he is about to say something but instead he slowly rolls to his side, pulling me tight to him as he does.

I'm burning up and his body isn't helping to cool down the heat but it feels amazing to have him wrapped around me and holding me. So amazing that my eyes fight to stay open. A fight I lose very quickly. I feel his lips against my forehead as he kisses me, and that is the last thing I remember before my body completely relaxes against his and I fall asleep.

CHAPTER
Seventeen

KAYSON

I HOLD Ashlyn as her breathing evens out and within moments she is fast asleep. My body hums for more of her, but I can guarantee that she didn't sleep at all when she got home today. I'm content to just lie her with her wrapped up tight against me and allow her to sleep. We have another shift in the morning and she has had a busy couple of days.

Kissing her on the forehead, I wonder why I denied myself this woman. If I would have manned up even after I left and just called her. No, this was supposed to happen now and now is perfect.

Kissing her forehead, my arms tighten a little more around her. "I love you, Ashlyn."

I give in to my exhaustion as well and fall asleep.

• • •

I HEAR the vibration and faint sound of my alarm on my phone going off somewhere in the room. Ashlyn hasn't moved from the position she fell asleep in, which just confirms how tired she was. We both have a shift today and as much as I would like to lie here all day long and have a couple repeats of last night, I still need to stop by my apartment and grab my stuff before heading over to the station.

My phone gets louder and Ashlyn starts to move. "What's that sound?"

"My alarm going off, we both have to work today."

She stretches next to me, her sleepy eyes looking up at me from where she is lying across my chest. "I would ask if last night really happened, but since I'm lying on top of you naked, I think that answers the question."

Her head is bent back as she looks up at me with a sleepy smile. Bending my head forward, I gently kiss her. "Any regrets?"

"No."

"What's going through that mind, Ash?"

She flips herself over and rests her arms on my chest, her chin on her arms. "What is going to happen at work now?"

"We are going to do our jobs and in between that, I may throw you into the engine and have my way with you, or maybe sneak into your room at night."

She pulls the hair on my chest, "Kayson, I'm being serious."

"Ouch...and you think I'm not?"

"I don't want this to be what everyone talks about all of the time."

"Ashlyn, it's not like we are going to be hanging all over each other all day. Will they talk? At first, yes, probably, but then it will become old news. Now if Neil doesn't stop hitting on you, we may have a problem."

"Neil's a nice guy."

"That may be, but he wants what is mine and that's not going to go well."

"All right, caveman, stop pounding on your chest."

My alarm is still going off and just getting louder. My phone is in my pants somewhere on the floor.

"I would like to lie here and continue this conversation, but that annoying beeping sound that is getting louder is just a reminder that we both need to get moving. I have to run by my apartment and grab a quick shower and my stuff."

Ashlyn pulls herself up with her arms and kisses me. "You could take a shower here."

"I could, but then neither of us will make it to work on time and that would definitely get the crew talking."

"Good point. Go home and take a shower." She rolls over, allowing me to get up.

She lies there, watching me as I dress.

After I slide my shoes on, I lean over the bed and give her one more kiss. "I'll see you at work."

"Let's see who gets there first."

"Well, if you don't get your lazy behind out of bed, it will be me."

She sits up, "All right, I'm up. Now get out of here so I can get ready."

With one more quick kiss, I say, "Bye."

I'M PULLING into the back lot of the station with only five minutes before shift starts. The guy I'm relieving is sitting in his car waiting on me to pull in.

"Sorry, little distracted this morning," I apologize as I step down out of my truck.

"No problem, I've been sitting here willing the tones to not go off."

"Busy night last night?"

Shrugging, "Define busy, for this place nothing out of the norm."

Grabbing my bag out of the back seat, I notice Ashlyn is already here.

"Well luck it be, you are free to go." I shut the door to my truck and make my way to the back door of the garage.

Walking inside, I head straight for my locker to drop off gear and of course, there are Ashlyn and Neil talking.

Walking past her I stop behind Neil, raising my eyebrow at her with a head nod toward Neil.

She gives me a slight shake of her head and that look that says I better not make a scene.

Neil notices our silent conversation and turns to me, "Hey, man."

Over his shoulder I see Ashlyn giving me that look that tells me I better not say anything to embarrass her. Who, me?

It's hard for me not to just take Ashlyn by the arm, pull her into me and kiss her right here in front of Neil, but Ashlyn would kick my ass if I pulled such a move.

"I need to speak to Ashlyn for a minute if you are good with that. Didn't mean to interrupt." I'm lying, I completely meant to stop their conversation.

"Oh, sure." He turns to Ashlyn, "I'll chat with you later." Then leaves the two of us alone.

Ashlyn is glaring at me. "Really?"

"What? I thought I behaved pretty well."

Her hands are on her hips and she is just glaring at me. I'm not a jealous type of guy, but something about Neil pushes at me every time and I don't know why. I know she isn't interested in him.

Grabbing her hand, I lead her to a little hall away from eyes. Turning, I grab her by the waist, pull her tight against me and claim her lips.

She sinks into my embrace and grabs the front of my shirt, holding me to her. I didn't get enough of her last night, this is going to be a very long twenty-four hours.

Perfect timing as always, the tones. Both of our arms fall to our sides.

"I swear they know." I kiss her quickly on the forehead.

"Probably for the best." She turns and leads the way out to get geared up.

CHAPTER
Eighteen
ASHLYN

IF I THOUGHT my first day was insane, today beats it hands down. The only thing I'm extremely thankful for is that unlike the first day, today I'm not trying to dodge a bad mood Kayson as well.

It's three o'clock and we are just pulling into the station from what I believe has been our fifth or sixth call. Small stuff but exhausting all the same. I'm getting the real feel for the job today.

Opening the door to the cab, I go to step out and there is no way I'm hearing it correctly. I swear I've heard the tones so much today, they must be just going off in my head.

Nope, it's not my imagination. Holly crap, again?

Plopping myself back into the seat, I look over and Kayson is actually smiling at me. No, he is laughing at me.

"Welcome to Station 26."

Rolling my eyes at him, I lay my head back and watch as the city once again passes by the window.

Pulling up on scene at a hotel, we jump out to see a man hanging from his foot that is stuck in the bars of the room's balcony, hanging upside down.

The captain signals our ladder truck to position itself, a police officer joins us.

"Why hasn't anyone tried pulling him up from the room balcony?" Cap asks the police officer.

"That guy hanging wasn't supposed to be in the room. Boyfriend showed up and is refusing to help him or open the door so that someone can. They tried from the room below, but the way his foot is stuck they were afraid he would fall."

"The man was going to jump from the fifth floor?" I asked.

"You haven't seen the size of the boyfriend, jumping probably seemed the better option. Hotel security is opening the door for our police officers now, it shouldn't be long."

"Striker, Murphy, you two are up." The captain orders us to be ready to climb up and unhook the man.

Striker and I busy ourselves with getting ready to make the climb, arial ladders were my favorite part in training.

I step up to start the climb when someone grabs my arm, stopping me.

"I'm going instead of Murphy." Kayson's voice is next to me.

"What the...?" I look over at him wide-eyed and pissed.

"I believe I told Striker and Murphy they were going," the captain repeats himself.

"What if the guy starts fighting them? It's safer if I go, more experience."

"Everyone on the crew has to be able to handle the job, Shaw. My orders stand."

Kayson looks at me and I'm pretty sure he can feel my pissed off stare that I am giving him down to his soul. What the hell does he think he is doing?

"Back off," I warn him in a low voice.

Kayson takes a couple of steps back, and I proceed to follow Striker up the ladder.

It takes Striker and myself all of maybe ten minutes to get the man down safely and unharmed, well, besides the broken ankle the man has from stopping his fall.

Stepping off the ladder, Kayson walks straight up to me. I stop him with a hand out in front of me before he can close the space between us.

"Stop."

"Look, I'm sorry."

"Now isn't the time, Kayson."

I have nothing to say to him right now. I don't want to even look at him.

We clean up, ready the truck and engine to leave and once again we are on our way back to the station, all of us hoping it quiets down for the evening.

Once the engine stops in the garage, I quickly jump out of the engine, drop my stuff off at the locker and head up to my room. I don't want to talk to anyone, least of all Kayson.

Shutting the door, it's immediately reopened. Turning, I find Kayson shutting it behind him.

"You are the last person I want to talk to right now, Kayson."

"Tough, we are going to talk. You're pissed, I get that."

"Pissed, really?"

Fine, he wants to talk, let's talk, then he can get the hell out of this room.

"Actually, no, I'm going to do the talking. Don't you ever do that to me again. What in the hell were you thinking? I thought you were different, I thought you supported me, I thought you believed in me and my ability to do this job. It took all of two seconds for you to show me how very wrong I was."

"Ashlyn, I'm sorry. I realized how wrong I was once I said it. It's a natural need to want to protect you."

"You act like it's something you have always had to do. Damn, Kayson, you and Jackson were gone all four years I was in high school and then I've managed to take care of myself the past three years alone here in California all while becoming a firefighter just like you. Passing all the same tests, probably working out and training harder because I need to keep up. I don't need you protecting me, I've been doing a damn good job of it I think for a while. I'm not the little girl that you two had to teach to ride a bike, or to swim any longer. I'm a woman, yes, but I'm a firefighter just like every man on this crew. You can't push me out of the way every time you think it may be too dangerous for me. I have to run into that burning building right beside you."

He is standing there, hands on his hips, his head hanging down. "Look, I'm sorry. I'm telling you what I did was wrong. I guess this having you climbing ladders and running into burning buildings is going to take a little longer for me to get used to and not have my instincts kick in to pull you back. I have no idea what else to say to you that will convince you of how sorry I am, how wrong I know I was."

I see the regret in his stance, but right now I just need to have a little space. "I believe that you're sorry, but right now I need you to leave. I just need some time to cool down."

For a moment I think he is going to stay, but then he turns and opens the door, shutting it behind him as he steps out of the room.

This room is small and I need some fresh air. We have some chairs set up outside and it sounds like the perfect place to go sit and think.

I get through the station without anyone really paying much attention to me. Walking outside, I take a deep breath and flop down in one of the chairs. Throwing my head back and closing my eyes, I relax a little more into the chair.

"You know the birds love to hang out over that ledge you are under. For your safety from any falling bird shit, you may want to change what seat you are sitting in, there have been many casualties in that chair."

Opening my eyes and not being able to help the smile from spreading across my face, I see Jeff standing over me.

"Thanks for the warning." Looking up above me, he wasn't kidding, there are two birds sitting there, I swear looking down and just timing their drop. I stand quickly and switch to the next chair.

Jeff sits down in the chair next to me and relaxes back. So much for a little time alone to think.

"Crazy day today."

I nod. "They weren't kidding when they said this place is insanely busy. They warned me at the academy when they found out what station I was going to, but I like it, makes the day move a little faster."

"That it does."

Silence stretches between us for a minute, but then Jeff sits forward in his chair, resting his arms on his legs. "Look, Ashlyn, I'm just going to say what I followed you out here to say, besides warning you about the birds."

"Which I appreciate."

"Kayson and I started here at the station on the same day. We became friends pretty quickly. Everything since that day, I can remember he has always been the most protective one of the guys on the crew."

I give Jeff my best "really" stare.

He throws up his hands in a surrender motion. "I'm not making excuses for him for what he did today, that was completely wrong and he knows it. You know, the moment I walked over the other morning and saw you standing there, I knew exactly who you were. Kayson has a picture of you and him together at his place."

That bit of information shocks me.

"Every once in a while, your name would pop up in conversation, but after seeing his reaction to you being here the other day what I always thought was confirmed. The man is in love with you."

"It's from knowing me most of my life, it's a sister kind of love."

Jeff is shaking his head, "No, it's not and you know it. You don't have to hide anything about the two of you from me. Guys don't talk about a woman who he looks at as a little sister the way he did about you."

I want to ask him what Kayson said, but I just let Jeff continue with his story.

"Look, all I'm saying is yes, what he did today was wrong, but go easy on him. It's hard to watch the ones you care about walk into something that can be dangerous and just stand there, when every bone in your body is screaming at you to stop it from happening. It doesn't mean he thinks you can't do the job, it means he can't live with himself if something were to happen to you and he knew he could have stopped it from happening."

"I'm a firefighter, Jeff, just like you, just like Kayson. I may get hurt, or worse, it wouldn't be anyone's fault, it's a reality we have to face being in this profession. He can't charge in every time."

"And he won't. He may slip every now and then, but he will learn to stand back. Just be patient with him. For a man, it's never easy to see the woman he loves walking into danger."

"I understand your point and I'm not really upset anymore. I just needed a little time and some fresh air."

Jeff stands up, but before he leaves he adds, "You did a great job today and handled yourself well with the situation."

I smile up at him. "Thank you."

CHAPTER

Nineteen

KAYSON

SHUTTING THE DOOR BEHIND ME, I decide the best thing for me to do right now is to give Ashlyn a little space. I could have groveled a little more, waited until she forgave me, but in all honesty she is right to be pissed at me. It was wrong for me to do what I did. I don't even know why I did it.

Walking down the short hall, I see the captain waiting for me. I put my hands up in a defensive position. "I know, trust me, I know."

"Kayson, what is going on? You can't keep having days like this."

"Not going to lie, this is going to be a lot harder than I thought."

"So do I need to have her transferred?"

"No, not at all. Plus, if I thought that would solve the problem I would have you move me to another station, not her. She hasn't done anything wrong."

"Moving her to another station isn't saying she has done something wrong, just means this station wasn't a good fit."

"Same thing, Cap. Look, after I said it, I realized how wrong I was today. I have apologized to her, I was on my way to talk to you and apologize to you for questioning your orders. I was completely out of line today and I can promise it won't happen again."

"Kayson, trust me, I know what it's like to want to protect family, but I've been watching the two of you and I know I have already asked this once the other day, but I feel I need to ask it again. Is there something more going on between you and Ashlyn?"

I could deny it. But there are no policies against it, so why would I lie about it? "All I can say is yes, our relationship has moved away from the friends only area, but I promise you, and I know today is not proving my point well, however, it will not interfere with our jobs."

"Maybe we should switch one of your shifts. Stay at the station, just move it around a little."

"I know I don't have the right to request this at this time, but I am going to anyway. I ask that you leave everything as is and allow me to prove that it can work out."

If he has either one of us change stations or shifts, any hopes of me having any kind of relationship with

Ashlyn will go out the door with which ever one of us leaves. Ashlyn will blame me.

Cap takes a moment to think about it. I can see him arguing with himself in his head. "All right, I will wait. Anything else, Shaw, and someone is moving."

"I understand, and thank you."

"You're a great firefighter, Shaw, I don't want to lose you from this team." With that he turns and walks away.

WALKING DOWN INTO THE BAY, I round to the front of the engine and sit down on the bumper. The doors to the garage are open and I just watch as the cars pass by the station.

Last night when I had Ashlyn in my arms it had finally felt like everything was right. I wasn't missing a thing. Funny how that ponytail-wearing little girl that would follow us everywhere would become the woman I couldn't live without.

"Mind if I join you?" Her voice is low.

Looking to my left, Ashlyn is standing there leaning against the corner of the engine. I pat the spot on the bumper next to me.

I wait for her to speak. She came looking for me, so she must have something to say.

We are both looking straight ahead, just watching the city as it passes by.

"It's crazy to sit here and watch the city drive by. I think of all the people who pass by and I wonder who will be the next one to try something crazy to set those tones off."

"You mean like try and jump off a fifth-floor balcony, but get their foot caught in the railing and end up hanging upside down?"

She laughs, a sound that strikes me right in the chest. "That man was so desperate to get out of that room, he was willing to jump. I bet he thinks twice before messing around with a woman who is already in a relationship. We never got to see the boyfriend, I would have loved to see what scared him so bad. Are we morbid for finding the humor in these calls?"

"Nope, if you don't find the humor, the ones that knock you off your feet will destroy you."

She turns her body toward me. "Kayson, I know in the world of relationships, man protects woman. I know in the line of work I choose to do, it's prominently a man's profession and this job is to protect. Everything around us is screaming for us to protect. I'm a firefighter, and I know what can happen to me in this line of work, but I love it. I love helping those who do insane things like jump off a balcony when they can't fly. I love watching as people are saved from burning buildings because there was someone who was brave enough to run in after them. I love soothing that child while their parents are receiving care. I need you to know, outside of this station, you are my protection. I feel safe in your arms. And while I'm here, I know you have my back, another security I thrive in and it helps me tackle the scary part of this profession, but you have to allow me to do this job, like you would anyone else on this crew."

I look from her back to the stream of passing cars. "The other day when it finally clicked in that you were wearing the uniform, it actually didn't surprise me. That you were standing in my station, here in California, that surprised me, but being a firefighter, no. You have always helped those around you. Remember that one time that kid fell on his bike in front of your house, you had no idea who he was, I don't remember what you were doing but you ran right over to him. Your instincts have always been to help."

"That boy tried to kiss me after that and I punched him. I was in junior high, I remember that day. You and Jackson were out working on his car, I was just watching from the porch. I already had a huge crush on you. I didn't want you seeing anyone trying to kiss me, just in case you liked me."

Now that she mentioned it, I do remember her punching the kid. "You've had a crush on me that long?" I ask in disbelief.

"I'm pretty sure I started crushing on you the moment I realized boys didn't have cooties."

Grabbing her hand in mine, I kiss the top of it. "Ash, I can't promise the protective side isn't going to come out of me when I see danger around you, but I will try hard to not move you out of the way, but make sure to have your back so that you don't get hurt. Again, I'm sorry about today. You are a great firefighter and I know you can handle yourself just as good if not better than anyone else on this crew."

"I'm sorry that I got so mad…"

"Stop there. You had every right to be pissed, don't apologize."

"You know, I spoke to Jeff a little earlier and he told me you have a picture of you and me at your place."

"I do. I've told you many times, I wasn't trying to forget you."

She pulls out her phone and shows me the picture of the three of us on her screen.

"Yes, but mine is just of the two of us," I state.

"Yes, and mine you are just lucky it doesn't have a mustache drawn across you face." She laughs.

Cupping my hand around her neck, I bring her in close to me. "I'm going to kiss you now and I really don't care who sees us."

"They are going to find out at some point." She closes the space between us and takes my lips with hers.

Shouts and clapping echo all around the garage as the crew above us cheers us on. Ashlyn pulls away laughing.

"Does this mean I'm forgiven?" I ask.

She leans over and kisses me again. I'm going to take that as a yes.

CHAPTER
Twenty
ASHLYN

I WAIT, because I know they won't disappoint. Over the clapping and hoots and hollers, there is the sound that can change our mood in a second. The tones, and there they are, right on time.

Over the speaker throughout the station we hear announced a large apartment complex fire, people trapped. Everyone starts making their way to their gear, kicking out of station boots, only to step back into work books and turnouts.

The engine and ladder truck pull out of the station, sirens blaring telling people to move. I can't put my finger on why but something feels different about this call. We have been to fires, we have had to pull someone out of a house on fire, but something runs a chill up my spine when I know people are trapped, but have no idea how many. An apartment complex is huge.

There's a hush throughout the cab amongst the crew, the only sounds are the sirens and the radio, updating as we make our way through the city.

Pulling up, the sun it just setting, but the blaze from the building is casting an eerie red glow throughout the sky through all of the smoke. Engines, ladder trucks, tillers, every type of fire vehicle has surrounded the building.

Flames are filling the space behind some of the windows, some have broken through and are licking the sky above. Water is being dumped onto this building from every angle. Paramedics are parked everywhere, some already working on those who have come out of the building, others waiting just in case.

One of the city's chiefs walks over to our crew, or more so our captain. "We have two crews inside and trying to locate tenants that aren't accounted for as of yet. We have a crew on the roof. I need your ladder up on the west side of the building, and a crew inside to help with rescue."

Our captain nods and turns to us, "Garcia, Seth and Neil, take the truck to the west side and start setting it up. Shaw, Cowboy and Murphy, suit up, you three are coming with me inside. Scott, you are on controls on the engine. Striker and Carter, you are on the hose down here."

Everyone begins to move in the directions we have been told to take.

Radios have been checked along with the air levels in our tanks. The four of us are ready to enter the building and start our search for anyone who may still be inside.

The chief meets us just before we enter. "They have already cleared up to four. I need you guys to assist on the fifth floor. We have a number of apartments that have people still in them."

The captain leads the way as we enter the building and make our way to the stairwell. The smoke is thick and visibility is very limited. I have Cowboy in front of me and Kayson behind me.

I know we trained for this. They throw us into a burning building and basically test our ability to find our way around and out. Put us into scenarios that prepare us so that we don't panic. Nothing could prepare us fully for this.

Once we have climbed the five floors of stairs, we enter through the door and make our way over to the crew going door to door.

They direct us over to the east wing of the floor. There is nothing to do but to start pounding on each door.

So far every apartment has been empty. Over the radio comes information that they have spotted an older lady, east side, waving for help from her window. We locate the apartment and try the door. It's locked. More information comes through. The lady is wheelchair-bound, lives with her daughter who was gone to the store and drove up to find the building on fire.

Cowboy takes a step back, turns around and back kicks twice before the door gives way. We all four enter and find the woman in her room, in her chair. The captain walks over, picks the woman up out of her chair and hoists her over his shoulder.

"Let's go," he orders us.

We backtrack the same way we came and just as we get to the stairwell, information comes over the radio again.

"Station 26, we have a sister trying to enter the building, says her twelve-year-old brother is in apartment twenty-three. She brought the dog out for a walk before the fire started, has not been able to locate him. Make one more sweep of the apartment."

"Cowboy, you are with me, Murphy and Shaw, go check out the apartment," Cap orders.

Kayson and I keep moving to the west side of the building where the other crew has already checked.

Approaching the door, it's still standing wide open from the initial search. Kayson leads the way in and together we start making our way throughout the apartment. The smoke is so thick it's hard to see. We run through each room, using our flashlights to look under the beds and in the closets.

"Shaw, Murphy, fire is on the floor above you, they just cleared off the roof, building isn't stable, any sign of the boy?" Our captain's voice comes over the radio.

"Sir, we have checked everywhere, is she sure he isn't down there?" Kayson answers back.

Looking around, I make a mental note of everywhere we have been. Just to make sure we haven't missed a popular or not so popular place for a kid to hide.

"Captain, do we have a name for the boy?" I ask.

"Name's Adam."

Kayson and I make an effort to yell out his name hoping he'll hear it and know we are here to help him, but nothing.

"Both of you, get out now." The captain's voice is loud in our radios.

"We've checked everywhere, I don't think he is in here. We need to head out!" Kayson is yelling as he makes his way to the front door.

Just as we step out, we hear the cracking sounds of lumber starting to splinter. Before we take two steps back toward the stairwell, a loud roaring sound fills my ears and the floor shakes under our feet.

I'm thrown to the ground and a weight is on top of me, keeping me from moving. I'm sure it's only seconds, but it feels like minutes that I'm plastered to the floor, with the anticipation that the floor under us can drop, or the roof above us can fall.

The weight is lifted off and something grabs my arm. Finally able to move, I turn my head and see Kayson standing and pulling me up with him. He laid on top of me when the ceiling started to fall.

As we both gain our footing, I look over and see flames attacking the walls of the floor we are on maybe ten apartments down.

Turning, we are about to run for the stairs when I hear something. Stopping, I wait and listen.

"What are you..."

I put up my hand to stop him. "I heard something."

"Ash, the building is falling down around us, there are lots of sounds."

Just as I'm about to agree with him, I hear it again. It sounds like someone pounding on something. I turn and start following the sound. On the opposite wall of the apartment we were just in is a door in the wall. Some apartment complexes have trash shoots. I go to open the door and it won't budge. That's when I hear it.

Along with the pounding is a voice on the other side calling for help.

"Kayson, someone is in here. I can't open it."

"Shaw, Murphy, are you two all right?" The captain's voice sounds concerned on the radio.

"Yes, we have found someone trapped in what looks like a trash shoot," I answer back.

The building is starting to make that eerie popping sound again and this time we need to be off this floor when it goes.

The smoke is so thick now I can't see anything. I can hear and feel Kayson moving alongside of me, and before I know it, he has the door open, the boy over his shoulder and the two of us turn to head back down the hallway to the stairs. The only sign that we are heading the right way is because the bright red glow is behind us.

We are just about at the door, when again the sound like something is exploding surrounds us and the floor starts to shake. Kayson stops me, throws the boy into my arms and then drops all three of us onto the floor, his body covering ours. Then everything goes black.

IT'S VERY distant at first, but I can hear my name being called over and over. My body aches, my back feels like a wrecking ball crashed into it. My senses are coming back as I can feel my gear being pulled off of me and cool air rushing over my skin as my shirt is moved aside.

Opening my eyes, I see Neil's face first.

"Her eyes are open. Ashlyn, can you hear me?" His voice still seems miles away, but I can hear him. Responding is something else.

Where's Kayson, the boy?

Frantically, I start trying to look around, but my vision is blocked by the guys on my crew and what looks to be a paramedic.

"Kayson?" I manage past my lips.

"He is in good hands," Neil assures me.

What does that mean, he is in good hands? Is he not all right?

"Neil, what's wrong with Kayson? Where is he?" I try to sit up, but strong hands hold me down.

"I'm fine, let me up." I try again with the same results, strong hands holding me down.

Another face appears in front of mine, this time it's the captain's, "Ashlyn, you need to relax."

"Why won't anyone tell me what's going on with Kayson? How about the boy?"

"Thanks to you and Kayson, the boy only has some bruising. He is already with his sister and on his way to the hospital to get checked out."

"Ashlyn, Kayson used his body to shield both you and the boy. When the ceiling came down, he took some hard hits. He is already loaded up into an ambulance and they are leaving as we speak to get him over to the hospital."

My chest starts to tighten. The commotion around me begins to blur as I lie here and try to remind myself that I need to breathe. The paramedic's face is in my line of sight now, I can see his mouth moving, but nothing is registering.

Kayson used himself to protect the boy and me. That doesn't surprise me. I think that's one of the reasons I stayed so calm inside. Was I scared, yes. The building was on fire, we were watching it come down around us, but I knew Kayson was there, and like any other time I'm around him, I felt safe.

Jeff appears in front of me. "Ashlyn, you need to come back to what's happening now. If you want to go and see Kayson, we need to figure you out first."

Not sure why his voice registers, but it does. Nodding my head, I blink a couple of times to keep the tears I can feel stinging my eyes from falling.

"Can you move your fingers and toes?" the paramedic asks.

"Yes."

"Does anything hurt when you do?"

"No."

"Back, neck?"

"No."

"Let's try and sit up." The paramedic takes my hands and assists me on sitting up.

My back is sore, I feel my face scrunch up as I move.

"Why the face?" the paramedic asks.

"My back is sore."

"That's probably from the tank you were wearing. It probably bruised your back when everything fell on you, but I think we should take you in and get you checked out just to be on the safe side." He gently pushes back on my shoulders, having me lie back down.

"Jeff, I want you to ride with her. Keep us updated on her and Kayson. We will finish up here and head over." Looking over at the captain, as strong as he is trying to sound when he speaks, I can see in his eyes he's worried.

The only positive thing I can think of in this situation is that with them taking me to get checked out, I'll be where Kayson is at, so that when I'm cleared I can be there for him.

IT TAKES over an hour for the doctors to get all of the x-rays that they want and to be convinced I am good to release. My back is going to be sore and bruised, I'm sure along with most of my body, but because of Kayson I am unharmed.

One of the nurses wheels me out to the waiting room where Jeff is sitting looking through his phone. When he notices us coming in, he quickly gets up and walks over to meet us.

I go to stand and wince from the pain shooting up my back. The more time that goes by and the less I move, the more my back screams.

Jeff grabs my arm and helps me to my feet. "I'm assuming nothing is broken."

"No, just going to be sore and probably bruised for a little while," I say between clenched teeth as I get to my feet. "Any word on Kayson?"

Jeff shakes his head. "Not yet."

Jeff walks alongside me and helps me sit down in one of the chairs, then takes the empty one next to me.

"How bad was he?"

"Cap, Cowboy and Striker are the ones who went back in for you guys. I was still over with the ladder truck. By the time I got over to the engine after hearing you guys were trapped, they already had you guys out and the paramedics where working on both of you. I know they moved pretty fast with Kayson to get him out and over here. We kind of stayed out of the way."

"They haven't said anything to you yet?"

"No, just that they are doing a lot of x-rays and tests. Hopefully we will know something soon."

Shivering, I tuck my hands between my knees. They had taken off my gear and probably cut off my shirt when they were looking me over at the scene, I came in with only my tank top on and slider shorts that I wear under my gear. They gave me a pair of scrub pants to wear home but it's freezing in this waiting room with only a tank top on.

"Let me see if I can get you a blanket or something, I don't have anything with me to give you." Jeff gets up and walks over to the desk.

He walks back to me. "Hey, I have to go up the hall to get you a blanket." He reaches into his pocket and pulls out my phone, handing it to me. "Walker thought you might want this. He grabbed it from the engine and gave it to me before we left. I'll be right back."

Someone needs to call Kayson's family, let them know what has happened. I met them a couple of times, but I have no way to contact them, but Jackson would be able to.

Pulling up Jackson's number, I hit the call button, put the phone up to my ear and wait.

"Hey, Ash." My brother's very familiar and right now very missed voice answers after only one ring.

All the tears I've been holding in come rushing to my eyes and flood down my cheeks.

"Ash, what's wrong?" Jackson's concerned voice comes through the line, but I'm crying so hard I can hardly breathe.

"Damn it, Ashlyn, talk to me."

Jeff walks back in holding a blanket. He sees me and rushes over, taking the phone from my hand.

"Ashlyn!" I hear my brother yell.

"Hello, this is Jeff Young, I'm a firefighter with Ashlyn."

"Jeff, this is Jackson, we've met. Is she all right?"

I can hear my brother's loud voice over the phone.

Jeff places the phone on speaker so that I can hear the conversation.

I'm trying to take deep breaths to calm myself down, but it hurts and that just fuels the tears more.

"Tonight we were on a call and to make a long story short, Ashlyn and Kayson were trapped inside as the building fell. Ashlyn is bruised and sore but Kayson we haven't gotten any information on as of yet. I rode here to the hospital with Ashlyn when they brought her in." Jeff wraps an arm around my shoulders.

"Shit, but she is all right?"

Taking a deep breath so that I can ease my brother's worry a little, I answer, "I'm all right. We need to call his parents."

"I'll take care of that and I'm booking a flight out now. Jeff, please make sure someone stays with her until I get there."

"Don't worry, her brothers here at the station will take care of her."

ANOTHER HOUR PASSES and finally a doctor walks in, just as the rest of the crew starts filing through the door.

"I'm going to assume you are all here for the firefighter brought in." The doctor looks around to the now full waiting room. Everyone on our crew came along to check how we were.

The captain takes a step forward. "I'm Captain Brett Mitchell, how is he?"

"Well, good news is that the only thing broken is his left arm, other than that I believe his gear saved his back and neck. On the other hand, he suffered a major blow to the head, even with the helmet on. He hasn't woken up and we are watching the swelling in his head. The next twenty-four hours are critical."

"Can I see him?" I start to stand up and have to hold from cussing out loud as my back is not happy with me.

Jeff is instantly on one side, Neil appears at my other arm.

"We are moving him to a room right now and getting him settled, probably best to wait until the morning," the doctor announces to the crew.

"I need to see him tonight," I insist.

The doctor starts to protest, but our captain steps forward. "She was with him, is there any way she can see him even if only for a minute? She is also the girlfriend."

The doctor looks over at me and gives an understanding smile. "All right, give us about twenty minutes to finish getting him settled in and I'll have one of the nurses come get you, but only for a minute."

"Thank you."

The guys all start talking around me once the doctor leaves. Jeff informs them that he will be staying because he promised my brother that someone would stay with me until he got here. Striker, takes his sweatshirt he is wearing off and gives it to me so that I don't have to keep the blanket wrapped around me.

A nurse comes in and lets me know I can follow her to go and see Kayson. Everyone tells me goodbye and Jeff and I follow the nurse back to Kayson's room.

"I can only allow one of you," the nurse explains when we get to the door of the room.

"I'm waiting out here, she is going in," Jeff tells the nurse.

Following the nurse in, she points to a chair over next to Kayson's bed. "I've been told I can allow five minutes."

"Thank you." I wait until she leaves the room.

The only sound in the room is the beeping of the monitor that is keeping track of Kayson's vitals. My breath catches in my chest when I finally look over at him and see him lying there, a breathing piece in his mouth.

Walking over, I grab the chair and pull it as close as I can to the bed and then slowly lower myself into it. Leaning over to him hurts, but I don't care, I need to be close to him. Taking his hand into mine, I squeeze, willing him to squeeze mine back.

"Kayson, you have to be all right. You saved me and that boy, but now you need to fight to save yourself. You promised me you wouldn't walk away from me again, I'm going to keep you to that promise."

I lay my cheek on his hand and just watch him, hoping that at any minute he will open his eyes, but he doesn't. I can't lose him now, I never told him I love him.

"Ash, the nurse says our time is up." Jeff places a hand on my shoulder.

I don't want to leave Kayson, but I don't want to cause a scene. They allowed me to see him, I have to respect the rules.

Jeff helps me out of the chair and I lean over and kiss Kayson on the forehead. "I'll be back in the morning," I whisper in his ear.

AS WE WALK DOWN the hall, Jeff answers a call. "All right, we will meet you out front."

I look up at him with a questioning look.

"Cowboy is coming to pick us up and take us to your place. The two of us will stay with you until your brother can get there."

"Jeff, you still have on your turnout pants. If we can get back to the station, I can drive my car home. I'll be fine."

"Yeah, right. Ashlyn, you can barely move. Like we are going to allow you for one, to drive and for two, to be alone. I promised your brother we would take care of you until he gets here. Cowboy is bringing me my bag, I'll change once we get to your house."

There is no use arguing. I'm not going to win.

. . .

I'M NOT sure what time it is, but the sun is beaming through the window of my room. Last night when we got here to my house, Cowboy and Jeff made themselves comfortable in my living room. I took a very long shower and managed to lie down in bed. I'm not sure what time I fell asleep or how long I've been out.

I can hear a deep voice coming from outside of my room, but only one and it's not Jeff's or Cowboy's. It's Jackson. He is talking but I don't hear another voice so he must be on the phone.

Slowly, I begin to sit up and realize my back is very stiff and sore. I don't care how much pain I'm in, I need to go and see Kayson.

I'm slow but I finally make my way out to the living room. Once Jackson sees me, he quickly ends the conversation on the phone, stands up from the couch and meets me, wrapping his arms carefully around me in a hug.

I appreciate everything Jeff and Cowboy did last night for me, but it is nice to have my brother here, it feels like home.

"Where is Jeff and Cowboy?"

"They left once I got here this morning."

"What time is it?"

"Almost noon."

"What? Why didn't anyone wake me? Have we heard anything about Kayson?"

"Calm down. His parents are at the hospital. I spoke to his dad about an hour ago. He hasn't woken up yet, but the doctors said he is responding to some reflex tests and that's all good signs. Mom and Dad will be here later tonight along with Hannah."

"They don't have to come, I'm fine." I go to sit down and the pain that shoots throughout my back takes my breath away.

"Yeah, you look perfect," my brother says in a sarcastic tone.

"I'm just bruised is all, I'm going to be sore for a little while. I want to go see Kayson."

"We all figured. That's why the guys went back to the station and drove your car back here so I had a way to get us back and forth to the hospital. Go get dressed and I'll drive us over there."

Jackson isn't saying it but I know he wants to be at the hospital as much as I do. It is killing him to be sitting here and not knowing exactly what is going on with Kayson.

EVEN THOUGH I was trying to hurry, we don't get to the hospital until almost two. Kayson's parents decide to go down to the cafeteria and grab something to eat since Jackson and I are both here.

Today Kayson doesn't have the tube in his mouth. I pull the chair up to his bed like I did last night and take his hand into mine. Jackson sits down on the other side of the bed.

"Second day on the job, Ash. That's all it took, two days."

I roll my eyes at my brother. "It's not like either of us wanted this to happen. We had to find the boy. Although I'm not sure why he was in the trash shoot."

"From what Jeff told me they found out, his sister had taken the dog out for a walk. He decided to be the twelve-year-old boy that he is and hide in it to scare her. The door jammed and with all of the commotion no one heard him, well, until you guys did."

"Not a smart place to hide."

"We don't think of that stuff at that age."

I look over at Kayson. "He handed me the boy, threw us both down on the ground and laid on top of me. He needs to be all right. We just found out that we kind of like each other."

"Kind of?"

Squeezing Kayson's hand, I admit, "Nope, that's a lie. I don't like him, I'm completely in love with him, even though he drives me crazy."

"In more ways than one." Kayson's raspy voice is low but he's talking clearly and when those blue eyes open and meet mine, I have to fight pretty hard not to cry.

I make the mistake of jumping out of my chair, but I push through the pain and take a deep breath. "Kayson."

"Buddy, remember, she is still my sister. Hospital bed or not, don't make me punch you."

Kayson gives Jackson a lazy smile and lifts his casted arm, to which my brother fist bumps.

Kayson's turns his head slowly back in my direction and squeezes my hand. "Did I just hear you say you love me?"

"You were supposed to be unconscious." I smile down at him.

"Doesn't matter, you said it, I heard it, can't take it back."

"I'm going to give you two a moment and go find his parents and let them know, and the nurse on the way back." Jackson pushes back his chair and stands.

Before he leaves the room, he turns. "Don't do anything to embarrass a nurse if they walk in while I'm gone."

He's out the door before I can respond.

Looking back down at Kayson, he is no longer smiling. His hand comes up and he brushes his fingers against my cheek. "How are you?"

Grabbing his hand, I kiss his palm. "Thanks to you, the boy and I are fine. I'm bruised up and going to be sore, but I'm good."

"I'm going to need you to do something for me."

I look down at him, puzzled. "Of course, what do you need?"

He pulls on my hand, bringing my face down to his. "First, I need you to tell me one more time that you love me and then I need you to kiss me."

"You know, a couple of days ago, I hated that I wanted you so bad."

"I know, I was a little bit of an ass."

I nod my head in agreement with him. "Yes, you were."

Closing the space between us, I kiss him gently. He isn't having anything to do with gently, though. His hand comes up around to the back of my head and buries into my hair, his lips demanding more than a gentle kiss.

Against my lips, he says, "Now about the I love you part."

Smiling, I push up just enough to see right into his eyes. "Kayson, I've been in love with you for half my life. I may not have always liked you, but I've always loved you."

"Ashlyn, I fell in love with you the first time I kissed you. I'm just sorry I waited for you to show up at my station to tell you."

"Better late than never."

Jackson chooses that moment to come back into the room. "Good, you are behaving. Your parents are on their way up."

"Actually, I was just telling Ashlyn that once we get back to the station, I'm going to have my way…"

I smack Kayson on the arm to stop him before he finishes that comment. "Really?"

"Man, you are pushing it," Jackson warns.

Kayson, still holding my hand, pulls me down and takes my lips in a kiss that probably makes my brother blush.

"I love you," he speaks against my lips.

"I love you, too.

CHAPTER
Twenty~One
KAYSON

TWO MONTHS LATER...

WALKING into the station for the first time since the apartment fire, I'm greeted with an empty garage. This morning before my shift I had a doctor's appointment to clear me, so I'm a little late for my shift.

Walking over to the lockers, I set my bag down on the bench and notice that Ashlyn has moved her locker next to mine. Jeff must have swapped with her, he has a soft spot for her. Next to Jackson, he is one of my best friends and I'm glad he was the one that stayed with Ashlyn when everything happened. Plus, I found out later, he and Ashlyn had a little talk that day and he was part of the reason she decided to forgive me for the asinine move I made earlier that day on a call.

I have new gear hanging in my locker. The gear I was wearing that night had been destroyed.

Its bright yellow color flashes me back to that night. I remember finding the boy, I remember hearing the sounds of the ceiling as it started to give way above us. My hand had just reached the frame of the door to the stairwell we were searching for so we could get out. We were only seconds too late.

I remember thinking I had to make sure Ashlyn and the boy survived. I spun Ashlyn around, tucked the boy into her arms, then pushed her down onto the ground, her body protecting the boy and then mine protecting hers. That's all I remember.

They kept me four days in the hospital to watch me before they finally allowed me to go home. Of course home was Ashlyn's house, she wasn't letting me out of her sight. A month into me healing, we both decided it was stupid for both of us to be paying rent when I was never at my place. Her house had more room than my apartment, so I moved in with her.

When she came back to work, she tried many times to have me just come on down and visit with everyone, but I decided this was the best time for her to find her place in the station and on the crew, without me right behind her. Of course, I have had Jeff watching after her.

My phone buzzes in my pocket. Checking it, I'm expecting it to be a text from Jeff, but I'm wrong.

Jackson: Well…

Me: I just walked into the station.

Jackson: Jeff won't forget?

Me: No

My phone buzzes again. Rolling my eyes at my best friend, I find this one is from Jeff.

Jeff: We are about to roll in.

Just as the text comes through, the garage doors start to open.

The engine is the first to start backing in and before it's parked, the back door to the cab flies open and Ashlyn jumps out. She is wearing her turnout pants and t-shirt, sexiest thing I've ever seen. She runs up to me and jumps right into my arms.

"You're finally here."

"Ash, you saw me this morning. Actually, you see me almost every day."

"The doctor cleared you, right?"

"Well, if he hadn't I wouldn't be standing here."

Everyone has joined us now and Jeff is taking his part in all of this very serious. He has made sure he is in front of everyone with the best spot. His phone is up and he gives me a nod that we are good to go.

Ashlyn turns around and sees everyone standing there. Taking advantage of her back to me, I pull the ring box out of my pocket and get down on my knee in front of her.

"What's going on?" she asks.

Cowboy signals for her to turn around.

She looks back at me puzzled, then her hands fly up to her mouth and tears are instantly springing up in her eyes, making them shine.

"Ashlyn, I can say that we have literally been through fire together and I made you a promise that I would never walk away again, I think the best way to prove it is to ask you to marry me."

Her head is bobbing up and down, tears are streaming down her face, but she manages a, "Yes."

Once the ring is on her finger, she launches herself into my arms and kisses me as if no one is watching.

The shouts and the cheers say otherwise.

Just like every time before, the timing couldn't be more perfect.

The tones go off.

"Let's go to work." I set her down on her feet.

The Engine Rolls Out

But then we have...

Shame
on Them

CHAPTER

Twenty~Two

HANNAH

THE LAST THREE years have been rough. My best friend moved to California to go to school and even though she was trying to tell me it had nothing to do with Kayson, I know it had a lot to do with Kayson.

What I don't understand is why in that three years she never reached out to him, or told him she was in town.

I'm not going to lie, today is her first day at her new job, she is starting her career as a firefighter. I'm a little jealous, I still have a year before I get my degree and start in the hospital as a nurse. One more year of working in the restaurant business, then I get to say farewell.

I was completely surprised when she told me about her chosen career path. Again, I would put money down it was partly because that was the same career Kayson was doing, but she denied that as well.

Today is her first day on the job and I'm trying so hard not to give in on the fact that I knew about one of the largest surprises.

Playing it off that I had no idea Kayson would be working at the same station that she would be at was hard. We don't keep secrets from each other, but I thought this one was best not to tell her. This is something that needs to happen, no matter how much she's been denying it.

This conversation is killing me. Trying to keep up the farce that I have no idea what's happening, or what's going on in my life right now, is getting harder by the minute. So many secrets.

It didn't take Kayson long, and I figured it wouldn't. I knew he liked her. As much as I wanted to kick his ass for breaking my best friend's heart, I understood why he did it.

It's been one day and he already can't keep his hands off of her.

"And that could be disastrous. Plus, he kissed me, but never said he wanted anything more." Ashlyn's voice brings me back to the conversation.

"Ash, I get it. You don't want your heart broken again, but neither of you are in the same place as you were three years ago. Well, actually I guess technically you are, but that's not the point, you know what I mean."

"Aren't best friends supposed to be on your side?"

"I am on your side. I'm telling you to go for the man you have been in love with since you were in junior high."

"I'll think about it, after I get some sleep and clear my head a little. Love you and miss you. You need to come visit."

"How many of those firefighters that you work with are good looking?"

"I believe to be a firefighter the rules state you have to be good looking."

"Then I will be visiting very soon."

"Night, talk soon."

"Don't fight it too hard, I mean make him work for it a little, he deserves that, but have fun. Night." I hang up, before all of my secrets I've been keeping from my best friend slams her all in one day.

"Really, any cute firefighters?" A pair of strong arms wrap around my waist from behind and pull me in tight.

Like my best friend, I too had a schoolgirl crush. Hers was with her brother's best friend, mine was with my best friend's brother. The only difference was she knew I had a crush on her brother, she always teased me and said that was the only reason I was friends with her, so that I could get close to him.

In all reality, Ashlyn and I were inseparable. I moved here to this little town my first year of junior high. We sat next to each other in homeroom. Being the first day, of course I was a little shy, but she started talking to me right away. We've been inseparable ever since.

"Do you want me to tell her that you have kept something else from her, not just the Kayson thing? Pull all the band-aids off at once kind of thing." I give Jackson a questioning look.

ABOUT A MONTH ago I was on the evening shift at the restaurant when I noticed Jackson and a couple of his friends having dinner at the bar.

I had walked up behind him to say hi when I overheard one of his friends, "I'm all for the little surprise on Kayson, but your sister."

Tapping Jackson on the shoulder, he turns and with an instant smile he stands, and wraps me up in a big hug.

Once my feet hit the ground again I look between the three in front of me, "So I couldn't help but overhear, what kind of surprise are you planning for Kayson?"

"Oh no, if I tell you, you tell Ash."

Hand up in a scout's honor salute, I declare, "I promise I won't."

Jackson eyes me over a couple of times, but then shrugs his shoulders. "Ashlyn just called and told me what station she will be working at."

"Yeah, she called me a little while ago with that information, so?"

"So, it just so happens that she will be working at the same station as Kayson."

THAT WAS the conversation that started so much and led us up to this moment.

"Well at least if I'm going to go down, you will be going down with me and don't think for a moment I won't throw you under the bus and tell her you knew about the whole Kayson thing as well."

"Do you have any idea how hard that conversation was to have with her, when her brother is lying in my bed, naked?"

"Hmm…" His lips are on my neck, nibbling their way down my shoulder, "You're the one that decided to answer her call."

"What was I supposed to tell her? Sorry, call me later, I'm making out with your brother?"

Jackson's hand slides down my waist, over my thigh and between my legs.

My back arches, pushing my backside into his hardness.

"I think we have been doing a little more than making out," his words are heavy in my ear.

Taking his hand with my own, I guide his fingers into my heated core, begging for some attention as I rub my backside against him.

His other hand cups my breast and squeezes my nipple between two fingers. Between his fingers inside of me, the others around my nipple and his hardness very close to a spot that I normally shy away from having anything near, but for some reason is creating a sensation I've never felt before and it's great, I'm about to lose my mind.

I don't know if I want to beg him to pinch harder, push in deeper or grant him permission to enter an area I would never considered a possibility before now. All I know is I want to beg for something.

CHAPTER
Twenty~Three
JACKSON

MY NAME FILLS THE ROOM, begging me and I have no problem answering all of it. I need to be inside of her before I explode. Her little backside has been teasing me almost to the point of losing myself.

Pulling away from her, I hear her moan of protest.

I roll her over onto her back, "I've got you, trust me, I'm not finished with you yet."

She smiles up at me, but when I bend down and take a breast into my mouth, her eyes roll back and her back arches into me, begging for more. Her fingers dig into my scalp a little more each time I nip at her nipple. Her hips are thrusting up toward me, pleading with me to fill the ache there as well.

Her legs spread wide for me to settle in between. I adjust myself so that just the tip of my hardness is inside of her. The heat radiating from her is begging for all of me.

"Jackson, please."

"Open your eyes, Hannah."

She does and there is that smokey-green color that I have found that mesmerizes me.

"I want your eyes the whole time. I want to watch as you take me, all of me, and as I send you over the edge."

She only nods.

I slowly fill her. She licks her lips and pulls her bottom one in between her teeth, I almost lose it right there.

Once fully inside of her, I hold there for a moment and enjoy the feeling of her surrounding me.

Hannah's legs wrap around my waist and her hips thrust up toward mine.

I can no longer wait. Pulling back, I thrust back into her, and then again. I can feel her body tightening around me and know she is close.

Her eyes close, I stop. "Eyes on me, Hannah."

They instantly fly open and I smile down at her.

She matches my movements and before long her body is pulling me in deeper and deeper with each pulse of her release and I can no longer hold onto mine. I thrust into her one last time and our eyes lock as our bodies find their release together.

. . .

THE SMELL of coffee is what finally has me even contemplating getting out of bed. The last month has been a little crazy.

The night I found out what station my sister would be working at, I was at Hannah's restaurant. She had come over just as I was telling the guys what was happening and my plans not to mention it to either Kayson or Ashlyn.

I had stayed until Hannah had gotten off work and then the two of us had a couple of drinks there at the bar.

All right, I had a couple more than I had already drank, and Hannah is so small it didn't take much for her to become a little more than tipsy.

I decided it was best that we leave our cars at the restaurant, neither of us were in a real great stage to drive. We got a car to come and pick us up and on the way to her place I think is the one moment I will never forget.

Here was my little sister's best friend. Sure, Ashlyn has told back when we were all still in school that her friend had a crush on me, but I was in high school, and she was in junior high. I just laughed it off.

Right before we pulled up to her house, she looked over at me and there was something there in her eyes. She was battling something within, but her eyes were bright blue, almost the color of blue flames.

We just stared at each other for a few moments. She then unhooked her seatbelt and in one quick movement, she was sitting on my lap. I even remember seeing the shock in the driver's eyes through the rearview mirror, and she just kissed me.

I'm such a guy...that's all it took. Well that, the amazing night that followed and the fact that we have had a great time matchmaking both our best friends. You never know what's going to bring two people together.

My phone vibrates with an incoming call. Reaching over, I grab it from the from the nightstand. Above Kayson's name is the time, damn, it's almost eleven. I never sleep later than seven, maybe eight on a good day.

Swiping over the green circle, I answer, "Hey, man, what's up?"

"Did I wake you?"

"Nope, just leaving for the gym actually." I pump my arm in the air trying to stretch the muscles from sleeping on it.

"This won't take long, but I wanted to talk to you."

"Sure, what's up?"

"Remember when I told you about kissing your sister and how it wasn't going to happen again?"

My sister has only been at the station for a day. Not going to lie, my best friend is smarter than I thought. I was sure it was going to take him at least a week to get over pouting and realize he still had something for Ashlyn.

"Go on," I try to keep from sounding happy. I mean I'm still her older brother and have to make it a little hard on him, best friend or not.

"I lied. Jackson, you are my best friend, we have been through a ton together and I don't want to do anything to jeopardize our friendship. You are like a brother to me, but I can't ignore my feelings for your sister either and I'm hoping you understand."

There are so many sarcastic comments I can say right now, but I refrain from saying any of them. I've known Kayson most of my life, the man is nervous right now.

"I'm not sure what has taken you so long. I figured it out the first time I visited you. You have the picture of you and her up in your living room. Single guys don't usually put pictures out of women they are going to have to explain to other women. Ashlyn is an adult and if she is willing to give you another shot then I'm good with it, I know she is in good hands. On the flip side, though, know if you hurt her, the best-friend-like-brothers card isn't going to save you."

Finishing up my call with Kayson, I hear Hannah's voice in the kitchen. It's definitely time for me to get my ass out of bed. Grabbing my pants off the chair next to the bed, I decide coffee first, then shower. The day is already shot, so I might as well take my time through the rest of it.

Walking into the kitchen, I start, "Won't believe who…"

Hannah throws her finger up to her lips, silencing me as I walk in. "Hey, I have to go."

Hannah puts her hand over the phone. "It's your sister."

I nod my understanding and make my way to the cabinet for a cup and some coffee, listening to the one-sided conversation.

"I'm at work, one of the waiters had a question."

Leaning a hip on the counter, I wait until Hannah is done talking to my sister. Part of me is ready to tell her what's going on.

"Ash, before I go, you need to go for it. It'll be worth it."

I hear my sister's voice over the phone but not what she's saying, but they shortly hang up.

"Go for what?"

"Well, it seems your best friend finally took his head out of his ass and asked her on a date."

"So I hear. He just called me, letting me know that he can't stay away any longer."

Laughing, I place my coffee cup on the counter and wrap my arms around her waist, pulling her tight to me. "Missed you this morning in bed."

"Well maybe if you would have actually woken up during morning hours I would have still been there. It's almost eleven." She points at the clock on the microwave.

"I know. I can't even tell you when the last time I slept in this late was. I'm sorry."

"Don't apologize, I figured you must be exhausted with all the secrets you are keeping."

"Again, not alone in these secrets you are talking about."

Lifting her up, I place her on the counter and move myself in between her legs. Her legs instantly wrap around my waist, just like I prefer them.

"You know, we decided not to tell Ash because we wanted to make sure this was something that was going to work out. It's been a month, and I'm still kind of liking you…"

"Kind of?"

She shrugs nonchalantly, then brings her hand up and gives me the so-so wave.

"Do we need to repeat last night to remind you?" I lean forward and kiss her lips.

"It's not the sex part I'm talking about, it's this sleeping in until eleven." She's laughing at me.

Picking her up from the counter, I carry her back to the bedroom. "I think I need to show you how nice it is to sleep in a little."

IT'S BEEN A LONG DAY. Yesterday Hannah and I decided that it's time to tell Ashlyn that we are seeing each other. Kind of makes it official. Today I hit the gym after shift and I decided that after sitting at the bench press for an hour and hadn't lifted a weight, I might as well head home.

It's weird how life ends up sometimes. Best friends, ending up with best friends, which are sister and brother, wait…this could start sounding like some kind of back woods set up. Laughing to myself, I pull into the driveway.

I expected some kind of phone call today, either from Kayson or Ashlyn about last night. I thought Ashlyn would at least text Hannah if not call her, but neither of us heard from them and today I'm sure they are back at the station. Hannah and I even stayed in last night and had a pizza delivered to her place and decided on watching a movie just waiting on a call, but nothing.

Throwing my truck into park, I reach behind the seat and grab my bag out of the back seat. My phone starts to vibrate.

Pulling it out of my pocket, Ashlyn's face fills the screen. About time. I swipe the green button…

"Hey, Ash."

She doesn't respond. I pull the phone away from my ear and make sure the call didn't drop. That's when I hear what I think is her crying.

"Ash, what's wrong?"

Still nothing but the sounds of her sobbing on the other end. I push the button for speakerphone so that I can see if she hangs up on me or not.

"Damn it, Ashlyn, talk to me." My heart is slamming against my chest and I feel helpless.

I want to call Kayson, but that would require me hanging up with Ashlyn.

"Ashlyn!" I yell into the phone, because there is nothing else I can do.

"Hello, this is Jeff Young, I'm a firefighter with Ashlyn."

"Jeff, this is Jackson, we've met. Is she all right?"

Someone is at least with her, but I still haven't been told what's going on.

"Tonight we were on a call and to make a long story short, Ashlyn and Kayson were trapped inside as the building fell. Ashlyn is bruised and sore but we haven't gotten any information on Kayson as of yet. I rode here to the hospital with Ashlyn when they brought her in."

"Shit, but she is all right?"

"I'm all right. We need to call his parents."

Ashlyn's voice comes through the phone and I finally take a deep breath. At least she is talking.

I'm trained in so many scenarios to handle a crisis situation. Taught by the military and the police department to not panic when an emergency strikes, but nothing prepares you for it being your family.

"I'll take care of that and I'm booking a flight out now," I'm searching through flights as I speak. "Jeff, please make sure someone stays with her until I get there."

"Don't worry, her brothers here at the station will take care of her."

Ashlyn is all right, so my first call is to Kayson's parents to let them know the little information that I have. I wish I had more to tell them, but I give them the flight information I just booked and assure them that as soon as I get more information I will let them know.

Next call is to my parents. Trying to convince both of them that Ashlyn is all right is a chore, as I'm quickly flying through my house grabbing what I need and getting to the airport in an hour for my flight.

"I promise, as soon as I get some more information I will call you guys. I spoke to her, she is all right."

"You know how your sister gets. She could just be telling you she's all right," Mom says over the phone, I hear the worry in her voice.

"Why couldn't my children decide on safer jobs?" I hear her mumble in the background.

First it was me leaving for the military, then home only to join the police department here, and then Ashlyn's shocking news to all of us that she was going to be a firefighter.

"Guys, I have to get going, I promise to call as soon as I can. One of the guys from the station is staying with Ash until I get there."

"All right, son. We can be on a flight tonight if we need to." Dad I can tell is trying to stay calm, Mom is freaking out enough for the both of them.

"Promise." Hanging up, I grab my overnight bag and head for the truck.

I'm just pulling out of the driveway when my phone rings throughout my speakers. Hannah's name flashes across the screen of the truck.

"Hey."

"Hey, are you done in the gym? I had a break and thought I would call and see if you ever heard from your sister of Kayson, I haven't yet."

"Actually, yes. Don't freak out, you are at work and she is fine."

"Jackson, that is a very shitty way to start a conversation, what's going on?"

"Ashlyn and Kayson had an accident at work. I don't know much of the details. I know Ash is all right, but Kayson they don't have much information on. I'm on my way to the airport right now."

"Shit," I hear Hannah talking with someone in the background.

"Hannah."

I wait, but I still hear her talking to someone.

"Hannah!" I yell into the phone this time.

"What?"

"Look, I'm pulling into the parking garage now at the airport. I will call you as soon as I get more information."

"I'm getting someone to cover my shift, I'll get a flight out as soon as I can."

"Just wait until I find out more information, I promise I'll call as soon as I get there."

"No. Ashlyn might physically be all right, but if something happens to Kayson, I'm going to be needed."

She's right. I have no idea what's happening with Kayson. "I'll see you when you get there."

I FINALLY PULL up to Ashlyn's place around six in the morning. Using my key, that at the time I had no idea why she gave it to me, but thankful now that I have it, I let myself in. Two guys are sitting in her living room, both knocked out.

Setting my bag on the floor, I recognize the one as Jeff.

Walking over, I tap him on the shoulder and kind of stand back. You ever know how someone does with being woken up.

He looks up at me a little puzzled for a moment.

"Jeff, Jackson, sorry I had a key," I explain to the half-awake firefighter.

"Hey, man, wish we were seeing each other under different circumstances. What time is it?"

"About six."

Our conversation has the other guy waking up now as well.

"I really appreciate you guys hanging around."

"This is Billy, or you can call him Cowboy, we do at the station."

"Good to meet you," Cowboy stretches his hand out to me.

"Nice to meet you as well. Again, guys, thank you."

"It's no bother.

THERE HADN'T BEEN MUCH of a change in Kayson through the night, and the guys had gone and brought back Ashlyn's car. I have spent the whole morning on the phone between Kayson's parents and my own.

Kayson's folks arrived around nine this morning and went straight to the hospital and have been keeping me updated.

Looking at my watch, it's almost eleven and I haven't heard a sound from Ashlyn's room.

I just hung the phone from Hannah letting me know that she will be here later today, when her door finally opens and Ashlyn, moving pretty slowly, comes out.

"Where are Jeff and Cowboy?"

"They left once I got here this morning."

"What time is it?"

"Almost noon."

"What? Why didn't anyone wake me? Have we heard anything about Kayson?"

"Calm down. His parents are at the hospital. I spoke to his dad about an hour ago. He hasn't woken up yet, but the doctors said he is responding to some reflex tests and those are all good signs. Mom and Dad will be here later tonight along with Hannah."

"They don't have to come, I'm fine." I watch as she flinches when she goes to sit down.

"Yeah, you look perfect," I give her a sarcastic tone.

"I'm just bruised is all, I'm going to be sore for a little while. I want to go see Kayson."

"We all figured. That's why the guys went back to the station and drove your car back here so I had a way to get us back and forth to the hospital. Go get dressed and I'll drive us over there."

WE DON'T GET to the hospital until around two. As much as Ash is trying to convince me she is fine, I see the pain etched all over her face. As much as I think she should be resting and taking it easy, I know nothing is going to keep her from being her at the hospital.

Still doesn't keep me from keeping a close eye on her as we sit here in Kayson's room. She looks worried and it's my job to take her mind off of it a little.

"Second day on the job, Ash. That's all it took, two days."

She rolls her eyes at me. "It's not like either of us wanted this to happen. We had to find the boy. Although I'm not sure why he was in the trash shoot."

I tell her the story that the guys had told me.

"Not a smart place to hide."

"We don't think of that stuff at that age."

"He handed me the boy, threw us both down on the ground and laid on top of me. He needs to be all right. We just found out that we kind of like each other."

"Kind of?" I give her a questioning look.

"Nope, that's a lie. I don't like him, I'm completely in love with him, even though he drives me crazy," she admits to me.

"In more ways than one." Kayson's raspy voice is low but he's talking clearly.

Ash jumps out of her chair at the sound of his voice. I'm up from mine when I see the pain shoot across her face, but hold back and watch as she takes a couple deep breaths and seems to be pulling it together.

"Kayson." Ash leans over my best friend and looks hopeful.

Nothing is being said, so I break the ice.

"Buddy, remember, she is still my sister. Hospital bed or not, don't make me punch you."

Kayson gives me a lazy smile and lifts his casted arm, to which I lightly fist-bump.

Kayson turns his head slowly back in my sister's direction. "Did I just hear you say you love me?"

"You were supposed to be unconscious."

"Doesn't matter, you said it, I heard it, can't take it back."

"I'm going to give you two a moment and go find your parents and let them know, and the nurse on the way back." I figure now would be a good time to give them a few minutes alone.

Before I walk out of the room, I turn, "Don't do anything to embarrass a nurse if they walk in while I'm gone."

IT'S BEEN A LONG DAY. I still haven't slept, but Hannah just landed and as much as Ashlyn didn't want to leave the hospital, I think she is ready for a little best friend time now that we know Kayson is out of the woods, per se.

I'm dozing off on the couch when someone knocks.

Mom and Dad got here a few hours ago, and after stopping at the hospital they decided to go back to the hotel and get some rest, it's been a long day for all of us.

Opening the door, Hannah is standing there, a bag in hand.

"Don't get this the wrong way, but you look terrible."

I stand to the side to allow her room to come in. "Thanks, babe, honesty is the key to all relationships."

She sets her bag down and looks around. "Where's Ash?"

"Shower. She's moving a little slower so it takes her a little longer to get through one."

Hannah's arms come up around my neck, "Then I should have plenty of time for this then."

She brings my head down to hers and kisses me.

It's been a long and somewhat stressful day and she feels amazing in my arms. My arms tighten around her waist and pull her tight to me, my lips demanding more from her.

The sound of a throat clearing has us jumping apart like two teenagers who were just caught making out by one of our parents.

"I'm going to assume you didn't say anything to her yet." Hannah looks over at me with a questioning look.

I shake my head, "Nope, I figured her best friend should have that pleasure."

"Chicken."

CHAPTER
Twenty~Four
HANNAH

"I'M THINKING there is something someone should probably start telling me, although the lip lock I found the two of you in pretty much says everything, so why don't you continue the story with how long this has been going on."

Ashlyn is standing in the doorway of her room. Before either myself or Hannah can say anything, she puts a hand up, "Wait...I think I need to sit down first."

Ash makes her way to couch and sits down very slowly.

I rush over to her side to help her, "Ash, are you sure you are all right?"

Ashlyn smiles up at me once she is seated, "Nice try, my friend, but we aren't talking about me first, I want to know what's going on here. That wasn't a friendly, so happy you made it here safe kind of kiss I walked in on."

"This seems like girl talk and a perfect time for me to go and grab a shower." Jackson dodges out of the room.

"Thanks, babe!" I yell after him.

"Babe?" Ashlyn's eyebrow lifts up in question, "Exactly how long has this been going on?"

"About a month…"

"A month? Why haven't I been told about this before catching you in my living room together?"

"We both thought it best to make sure this was something that was going somewhere before we told you it happened."

"How much longer where you guys looking at waiting before you said anything?"

"Believe it or not, yesterday we decided after we both got off the phone with you and Kayson. You two have amazing timing when you are calling the two of us."

"So it was Jackson's voice I heard when I called yesterday?"

"Are you good with this?"

"What I'm not good with is the fact that you guys haven't said anything, but you two being together, I'm perfectly fine with. I really hope this is it for secrets, though. It's been a long week and I've had my fill."

"I promise it's the last one. I really want to hug you, but I don't know how without hurting you."

Ashly leans forward and wraps her arms around me. "I'm so glad you're here, it's been a blaze of a week."

The End

Tonya Clark lives in Southern California with her hot firefighter hubby and two amazing daughters. She writes contemporary romance featuring second chance, sports, MC, shifters, suspense, and deaf culture-inspired by her youngest daughter.

When not hiding in the office writing, Tonya has the amazing job of photographic hot cover models, coaching multiple soccer teams, and running her day job.

Tonya Believes everyone deserves their Happily Ever After!

Sign-up for Tonya's newsletter at www.tonyaclarkbooks.com for book news and you can find all of her books on Amazon.

facebook.com/tonyayclark

twitter.com/AuthortonyaC

instagram.com/authortonyaclark

amazon.com/author/tonyaclark

bookbub.com/authors/tonya-clark

goodreads.com/authortonyaclark

tiktok.com/@authortonyaclark

Also by Tonya Clark

Sign of Love Series

Silent Burn

Silent Distraction

Silent Protection

Silent Forgiveness

Sign of Love Circle

Shift

For the Love of Brayden (Releasing Summer 2022)

Standalone

Retake

Entangled Rivals

Driven Roads

Healing Tristan

Slide Tackled (Releasing Spring 2022)

Hidden Flight (Releasing Fall 2022)

Anthologies

Storybook Pub

Storybook Pub Christmas Wishes

Made in the USA
Columbia, SC
11 February 2024

31197423R10109